IN FOR THE KILL

A TANNER NOVEL - BOOK 47

REMINGTON KANE

Year Zero

INTRODUCTION

IN FOR THE KILL – TANNER 47

An unexpected event forces Tanner to struggle to survive.

ACKNOWLEDGMENTS

I write for you.

—Remington Kane

1

NO GOOD DEED

Tanner was on a small boat off the coast of Maine with his apprentice, Henry Knight. There was an open contract on a man named Alex Bergman. Bergman lived on a private island that was several miles from the coastline. Other islands were nearby, but they were much smaller and uninhabited. There were over four thousand islands off the coast of Maine; many were so small they had never been assigned proper names.

Alex Bergman's island was called Driftwood because the currents had a way of depositing debris upon its northern tip. That included the belongings of hapless tourists who overturned their boats during the summer months. Sometimes the boats themselves found their way to the island, and the debris created a mound. It was home to black-backed gulls who liked to nest there.

The island was also the location of an old stone lighthouse. The lighthouse had been out of use for decades. The inner wooden spiral staircase that once reached the top had crumpled many years ago, as had the house that had provided shelter to the lighthouse keeper. A newer lighthouse was in operation on a different island. Its modern arrangement of lenses produced a beam that was the equivalent of five million candlepower.

Tanner and Henry were out in the early morning hours doing recon on Bergman's defenses. Bergman's life was worth half a million dollars. One assassin had already attempted to collect the fee for killing him. That man had died at the hands of Bergman's defenders, after failing to kill his target.

Tanner had that information thanks to his friend, Raymond "Crash" Wyman. Crash was obsessed with assassins and kept track of their activities. The assassin who had died showed promise of being better than average, but he had bitten off more than he could chew when he went after Bergman. The price of failure had been paid with his life.

Tanner decided to go after Bergman because it would be a good training opportunity for Henry. Bergman's island getaway was far from impregnable, but it was well-guarded and would require an assassin to come up with a shrewd and careful plan to be successful.

Killing Alex Bergman was only half of the assassination; the other half would be surviving long enough to get off the island.

Successful assassins weren't Kamikaze pilots. Once your target was dead, it then became your job to keep yourself alive. The assassin who had recently been unsuccessful at killing Bergman had failed miserably at both tasks. His target still lived, and he had likely wound up being buried on the island or weighted down with rocks and given a watery grave.

TANNER AND HENRY WERE DRESSED ALIKE IN DARK BOOTS AND clothing. Their jackets were reversible, and the hidden sides were of a much lighter fabric. Once they were done skulking around and gaining intel, they would reverse the jackets, so they didn't look like a pair of cat burglars out on the prowl.

Tanner used a camera to take photos of Bergman's island. The expensive camera could record in night vision mode and had zoom capability. Henry had a scoped rifle; it was his job to scan for threats as their boat bobbed in the water off the island's coastline.

They both spotted the guards walking along the shore. The men were using flashlights and looking down at the sand for a sign that anyone might have recently passed by. If they came across fresh tracks in the wet sand, they would know that someone had come onto the island. That someone would then be hunted down and killed.

Alex Bergman had made his fortune in human trafficking. His specialty had been the exporting of young American women. Many had still been girls, as most of Bergman's victims had been between the ages of sixteen and nineteen. Bergman had become rich off their suffering and increased that wealth by investing well.

He had retired from his role as a modern-day slaver two years ago without ever having come to the attention of the authorities. Months earlier, his name had been mentioned by a former competitor of his who had been arrested and was looking to make a deal for leniency. The man claimed to have proof that Bergman had been involved with trafficking women, and the authorities believed he was telling the truth.

Unfortunately, the police didn't act fast enough to make a deal with the man; he was murdered while out on bail. Any proof he might have possessed went to the grave with him or was destroyed in a fire. The man's home had been burnt to the ground along with the homes of his brothers, and the building where he'd once had office space.

Bergman had learned about the snitch's plan to feed him to the cops for a lighter sentence. Bergman gave him that lighter sentence, that is, he used a cigarette lighter to sentence the man to death by setting him on fire to keep him from talking.

Being retired from a life of crime, and with a total lack of evidence or reputable witnesses against him, there was no way to bring Alex Bergman to justice. Fortunately, there were others who knew the truth about Bergman. Although they'd never become a snitch and talk to the cops, they did talk to others involved in crime and knew who was doing what. One of those people was New York City mob boss, Joe Pullo. Pullo confirmed to Tanner that Bergman had been involved with trafficking girls. Once Tanner had established that fact, he was willing to take the open contract hanging over Alex Bergman's head.

Henry would be helping him and would gain valuable experience. The contract on Bergman would be the toughest one Henry had ever been involved with. And while he wouldn't be pulling the trigger, he would play a key role in helping Tanner to escape the island after the contract was fulfilled.

UPON RETURNING TO THE MAINLAND, THEY DOCKED THEIR small vessel inside a private boathouse. They were staying in a home Tanner had rented under a phony identity the elite hacker Tim Jackson had created for him. Tim was providing other assistance as well.

The owners of the beachfront home had asked for an exorbitant fee that kept most vacationers away. It was the end of April and not yet beach season, that also contributed to the home being available.

Tanner and Henry were using two vehicles. One was a van and the other a car. If one of them left the property alone, the other would still have transportation.

After securing the boat, they took the van and drove toward the nearest highway. They were hungry and had decided to eat at a diner that was open all night.

The place was crowded considering that it was around three a.m. There were long-haul truckers mixed in with those who had closed down the bars. Two hungry hit men went unnoticed.

A rowdy group in a corner booth were drawing attention to themselves. They consisted of three men and a young woman. The woman was an attractive blonde with long hair and large blue eyes. Tanner had noticed that she looked at Henry more than once.

Henry had recently turned twenty. His full beard made him appear a few years older than that. He was taller than Tanner, carried a bit more muscle, and had a confident manner that had been well-earned. It wasn't unusual for women to be attracted to the young man.

Henry had noticed the blonde, as well as the man who had an arm draped over her shoulders, and his two friends. The woman was quiet, but the men were loud. It was obvious they had been drinking.

The group left the diner first. As they walked past their table, the blonde smiled at Henry. Henry sent her a nod in response. The woman's husband had seen the exchange and his face had grown dark with anger.

TANNER AND HENRY LEFT THE DINER TO FIND THAT THE GROUP from the corner booth were still out in the parking lot. The man and the woman were arguing. When the man spotted Henry, he jabbed a finger in his direction.

"Do you have something going on with him?"

"No. I don't know him, Billy. All I did was smile to be friendly."

The man grabbed her left arm with enough force to make her wince in pain. "Tell me the truth, Gabrielle. Have you been cheating on me?"

"No!"

Tanner spoke to Henry in a low voice. "Ignore them and get in the van. We don't need to attract attention."

"I don't like the way he's treating her."

"Neither do I, but it's not our business. She's a grown woman and—"

The sound of a loud slap made Tanner stop talking. The man named Billy had struck the woman hard across the face.

Henry was headed toward the group before Tanner could stop him.

"Hey! Asshole. Don't go around hitting women."

Billy looked Henry up and down. He and Henry were about the same size, but the man was a dozen years older, as were his two friends. The three of them converged on Henry and Billy spoke to him.

"Have you been screwing my wife?"

"I've never seen her before."

"Then why did she smile at you?"

"Maybe she was glad to see a real man, instead of one like you who beats on women."

Tanner walked over to join Henry. One of the man's friends looked at him and swallowed hard. The guy may have been drunk, but he knew a threat when he saw one.

"Billy, why don't we just go home. There's nothing going on between Gabrielle and this kid."

Billy took off the jacket he was wearing and handed it to his friend. "Hold this. I'm going to kick this guy's ass."

Tanner looked around. The traffic on the street was sporadic and no one in the diner had noticed what was going on outside. Walking away was no longer an option. If they did that, the jealous man would only escalate things. Tanner spoke to Henry.

"The man is looking for trouble; make sure he finds it, and then we need to get away from here."

"This won't take long."

Henry was right. Billy threw a punch at his face that he ducked, then Henry moved in a blur to deliver several shots to Billy's face and midsection. Billy's bottom lip was bleeding as he dropped to his hands and knees to barf up the meal he'd just eaten. The friend who wasn't holding Billy's jacket attempted to strike Henry on the chin. Henry leaned away from the punch then kicked the guy in the face, causing more blood to flow, as the man's nose broke.

The other friend, the one who had tried to talk sense into Billy was holding up his hands.

"I'm not fighting. Don't hit me."

"Let's get out of here," Tanner told Henry.

They were at the van when the blonde, Gabrielle, ran over to Henry before he could get in.

"Hey, mister. Hold on."

Henry turned to face her, expecting to hear words of thanks. When she moved closer, he wondered if he were about to receive a kiss of gratitude. Instead, he took a knee to the groin.

"That's for hurting my husband, jerk."

Henry slid into the passenger seat while moaning.

Gabrielle's knee had made contact with a sensitive area. When the pain diminished, Henry sighed, then spoke.

"You were right. I should have minded my own business."

"I might have responded the same way after he slapped her. What I wouldn't have done was let my guard down around that woman. Remember, anyone can be a threat."

Henry moaned again as he adjusted his position in the seat. "I'll remember that from now on."

Tanner smiled. "I bet you will."

2

CANCEL THE CONTRACT

ALEX BERGMAN ROSE FROM BED AFTER ONLY FOUR HOURS OF fitful sleep. He'd been in precarious situations before and had survived being in danger, but he'd never had to live in constant fear for his life, as he did now.

Someone wanted him dead and were willing to pay good money to see that it happened. He didn't know who had taken out a contract on him, only that his life was worth half a million dollars to whomever killed him.

Given the number of men guarding him, he'd been mildly concerned by the threat against him until an assassin had come onto the island a week earlier. That man had been shot dead, but he had nearly made it into the house. If he had gotten inside, Bergman assumed he would have been killed, since he had been asleep in his bed at the time.

The list of people who might want him dead was a long one, but fortunately, few on that list could afford to spend half a million dollars to bring about his death.

His chief of security and best friend, Michael Donahue, was searching for the person behind the contract. The working theory was that it was the father of one of the girls he had abducted and sold into sexual slavery.

That was not a short list. Bergman had been responsible for hundreds of girls becoming sex slaves. Other than selling drugs, it was the most profitable business one could be in, that is, if you were criminally minded.

Bergman had been a criminal since he was a boy. He started as a thief who robbed houses, moved into transporting illegal drugs, and made his fortune by selling girls.

Breaking into houses had been dangerous and barely paid his bills. Transporting drugs had been profitable but oh, so risky. He had come close to being busted by the law four times while dealing with drugs. During that last close call, he'd escaped by killing the cop who had searched his vehicle. He had knifed a motorcycle cop to death in Nevada along a desert highway after the man had uncovered the fifty kilos of heroin he had hidden in the walls of a van.

The van was later crushed into a cube in a junkyard after the heroin was removed. The cop's body had not been removed from the van, nor was his corpse ever found.

After that close call, Bergman decided to get into a different field. It was Donahue who suggested they become sex traffickers. Girls were easy to acquire, and the law wasn't focused on it like they were with illegal drugs.

More than a trillion dollars had been spent on the "War against drugs" but considerably less was spent to prevent human trafficking.

Also, if you were discovered with a kilo of heroin there was nothing you could say to talk your way out of it. If you were found with a girl and she denied anything was wrong, there was little the police could do. It wasn't against the law to drive around with teenagers.

As for the girls, they had been warned that talking to the cops would end in tragedy. If they talked, someone they loved would be killed; that someone might be a parent, a sibling, or themselves.

Bergman moved toward the balcony, but then he remembered he couldn't sit out there anymore. If he did so, he would be risking death from a sniper.

He cursed in frustration at being a prisoner in his own home. He also hated living with the constant worry that someone might place a bullet in his head.

Needing to burn off his nervous energy, he went downstairs to the room where he had set up a home gym. He wasn't a fitness fanatic, but he liked to stay in shape. That had been difficult to do as of late because he tended to overindulge in sweets and wine when he was worried. The home gym had a treadmill, a selection of free weights, and a sauna. Despite using the equipment on a regular basis, Bergman had gained twelve pounds with his overeating.

He worked out with the weights for a little while then ran on the treadmill. Afterward, he moved into the sauna and relaxed. The heat felt good and soon his eyes closed as he drifted off to sleep. When he awoke, his friend, Michael Donahue, was staring at him from the door of the sauna.

Donahue was the same age as Bergman, thirty-eight. The two had met in a Southern California high school at sixteen and had become friends when Bergman gave Donahue an alibi.

A teacher named Jenkins had been beaten into unconsciousness in the parking lot by someone wearing a ski mask. Jenkins had been disliked by many of his students because he had a habit of making fun of people. The fool had picked on Donahue, because Donahue was having trouble following along with the epic poem, Beowulf, which Jenkins had been teaching. He had insinuated to the class that Donahue was dim-witted. It wasn't true. Michael Donahue wasn't slow, he just looked less intelligent than most because of his sleepy-eyed gaze and his huge size.

It was his size that made the teacher and the principal assume Donahue had been the brute behind the ski mask. Earlier that day, he'd been red-faced with anger by what the teacher had said about him in front of the class. It was assumed that Donahue had acted on that anger to attack Mr. Jenkins.

Bergman didn't like the teacher either; he was glad someone had kicked his ass.

"Mike couldn't have beaten up Mr. Jenkins," Bergman had told the principal and the cops that had shown up. "He was with me when it happened."

The principal doubted his word at first, but soon accepted that he was telling the truth. Although he was a thief, no one knew of his extracurricular activities. As far as the school was concerned, Alex Bergman was an average student who had never gotten into trouble, nor had he and Michael Donahue been friends. He had no reason to lie to protect Donahue.

That was all true, and Bergman himself didn't know why he had stuck his neck out to help the big kid, but he came to be glad he had. Donahue stayed out of trouble and Bergman had made a new friend. To his surprise, he and Donahue got along great. They were both the only child of single parents. Bergman's mother was an alcoholic who lived on welfare. Donahue's mother was a prostitute and crack addict. The two had grown up neglected.

At sixteen, Donahue had already reached his current height of six-foot-three and was over two hundred pounds of muscle. Even then he was working as a bodyguard of sorts. The kid in their school who sold weed and pills had been mugged by two of the players from the football team. Donahue had kicked their asses. The drugs they'd stolen had already either been sold or used, but Donahue had made them pay back what they owed, and no one ever bothered his employer again.

Bergman had drifted into the drug business after high school. Needing protection from rivals, he had hired Donahue. The two had been together ever since, and Donahue had killed to protect Bergman on three occasions. He was the only one in the world that Bergman trusted, and that trust was mutual.

DONAHUE TOSSED BERGMAN A FRESH TOWEL. "DID YOU FALL asleep in here again?"

Bergman stifled a yawn as he wiped sweat from his face. "What time is it?"

"It's almost eight o'clock."

Bergman stepped from the sauna room and grabbed a robe. After being inside the sauna for so long, the air outside of it felt chilled.

"I think I'm going stir crazy inside this house. Are you any closer to figuring out who wants me dead?"

"I've narrowed it down to four possibilities. Three of them are the wealthy parents of girls we've sold. The fourth one is Lou Lazio."

Bergman had opened the door of his home gym to head toward his bedroom. He stopped moving with his hand on the doorknob and stared at Donahue. "Lazio? Why would he want me dead?"

"The fool is dating a girl from a good family who knows nothing about his past. Like you, he was successful in avoiding the law and maintains an appearance of respectability. You're one of the few people who know about his connection to human trafficking and can prove he was involved."

"Okay, but Lazio knows I would never talk to anyone about that. If I did, I'd be implicating myself."

"I don't think he wants to take that chance."

Bergman continued to his room. Donahue followed him inside and took a seat in a chair that was near a sofa and coffee table. The room was large and more like an apartment. It had a connected bathroom, a walk-in closet, a wet bar, and a kitchen area.

Bergman entered the closet and came out holding the clothes he would wear.

"The person that wants me dead must be one of the three parents you mentioned. I can't believe Lazio would be stupid enough to come after me for no reason."

"He has a reason. Like I said, he fears you'll talk someday. If that happened, that girl he's with would leave him in a heartbeat; her family would make certain of that."

"But why are you so sure it's him and not one of the parents?"

"Those people have the money to hire a hitter, but how would they have found out about you? Lazio knows about you already, and Alex, I think he's had other guys killed too."

"Like who?"

"Dave Vasquez is dead, and so are Nick Thompson and Jorge Ferraro."

Bergman was drinking a glass of orange juice. He lowered the glass and stared at Donahue. "Jorge was Lazio's partner at one time."

"That's right, and Dave Vasquez laundered his money, while Nick Thompson was in charge of moving the girls. Lazio is cleaning house."

"How did they all die?"

"Vasquez was killed in what the cops are calling a

mugging. Nick Thompson went out on his boat one day and never came back, and Jorge was found shot to death in his home."

Bergman sat on the side of his bed. "Lazio, that son of a bitch."

"I say we fight fire with fire and hire a hitter to take him out. Once he's dead, the contract he put out on you will go away."

"It will, won't it? And that means I'll no longer be trapped in this house and will be able to leave the island. But how do I go about hiring a hitter?"

"I know how. We'll make it an open contract, just like he did with you. That way, more than one hitter will be going after Lazio."

"But what if one of his hitters gets to me before one of mine gets to him?"

"The sooner you put out the contract the better. And unlike you, Lazio doesn't have an island to hide on. He'll probably be dead within a week."

"But won't the contract still be out there even if he's dead?"

"Maybe, if he used a middleman. If so, then the contract will remain in effect. I'll find out who the middleman is and have him put down."

"Damn Lazio! He's forcing me to spend good money to kill him."

"It won't cost you a cent if I can get Lazio's money away from the middleman. And because he'll also be holding other people's money, you might even make a profit."

Bergman stood and headed toward his bathroom. "I'm going to take a shower. Handle everything for me, will you, Mike?"

"Don't I always?" Donahue asked.

Bergman turned and smiled at him. "Hell yeah, you do.

Take half of anything you get once you find the middleman, even if it's only the money from Lazio."

"I'll do that," Donahue said, as he watched Bergman disappear into the bathroom.

Neither man was aware that their conversation had been overheard by a third party.

3

A NAME FROM THE PAST

TIM JACKSON HAD MANAGED TO REMOTELY ACCESS MICHAEL Donahue's satellite phone. Any conversation Donahue had on the phone or near the phone was automatically recorded by Tim.

When he heard Bergman and Donahue discussing Lazio, he sent Tanner a copy of the conversation.

"It sounds like Bergman is trying to cancel the contract on himself by taking one out on the man who wants him dead," Tim told Tanner by phone.

"I don't know who took out the contract, but it sounds like Donahue might be right about Lazio."

"What are you going to do if the contract is withdrawn?"

"I'm not sure. It's an open contract, so I could just walk away if that happens."

"Too bad."

"What do you mean?"

"Bergman is a scumbag of the highest order. The man kidnapped girls for a living and sold them into sexual slavery. I'd hate to see him live happily ever after, you know?"

"I hear you, Tim. But if I spent my life going around

killing every scumbag there is, I wouldn't have time for anything else. But don't worry, I'll be killing Bergman soon. Now that we know what Donahue is up to, we'll be able to stop him."

"Do you know who the middleman might be?"

"There are only so many people acting as brokers between assassins and their clients. I'll have someone find him and then I'll stop Donahue from killing him. If the middleman stays safe, the contract remains in force. As for Lazio, he's on his own."

"It sounds like he's as big a scumbag as Bergman," Tim said, then he laughed. "Maybe you should take that contract too."

"You know, that's not a bad idea."

"Seriously?"

"Yeah. But before that happens, I need to locate the middleman, or someone will put him out of business permanently."

TANNER CALLED KATE BARLOW. IF ANYONE COULD TRACK down a middleman who brokered deals for assassins it would be her and her husband, Michael.

Kate sounded pleased to hear from Tanner and asked him how Sara was doing.

"She's gone back to work, as a bounty hunter. She and a friend of ours captured two men the other day who were wanted for child molestation."

"That's great. How can we help you?"

Tanner explained what he needed, and Kate said she would get right on it.

"Michael and I have been sitting around and doing nothing for over a week; it will be good to get back to work."

"Be careful, Kate. The person you're looking for won't be happy that you've found them, and they're someone who works with assassins. If you get on their radar, they may send a hitter your way."

"We'll be careful, and I'll try to be quick about it."

"Thank you."

"Anything for you, Tanner; you know that."

TANNER TEXTED HENRY. THEY MET IN THE LIVING ROOM TO discuss what Tim had learned.

"A middleman? Didn't you tell me that you used to work with one years ago?"

"I've worked with several over the years, and so has Spenser. With the internet, most assassins can stay anonymous on their own now, but back when I started, it was helpful to have a go-between."

"What are you going to do once the Barlows find the person you're looking for?"

"I'll let them know they've become a target."

"I wonder if Crash knows anything about go-betweens."

Tanner took out his phone. "He just might. That's good thinking, Henry."

WHEN CRASH WAS ASKED ABOUT THE CURRENT CROP OF middlemen, he told Tanner he could help him.

"There aren't many of them anymore, as most assassins prefer to do things themselves, and there are only a few that would handle a contract worth half a million dollars."

"I know you keep track of assassins, but do you know

19

how I might make contact with the go-betweens who handle large contracts?"

"I can give you that information. But as of late, there's only one contract in the half a million range being offered, and it's on Alex Bergman."

"I don't know how much Bergman will be offering for the man he thinks put a contract out on him, but I doubt it will be anywhere near half a million. If you hear about the contract and can identify the go-between who brokers it, let me know."

"Won't that be the same man who's handling the contract on Bergman?"

"Not likely. Bergman wants the man brokering the contract on him dead. Once that man dies, any contracts he's involved with get nullified. If he used that same man to put a hit out on Lazio, when the broker died, the contract on Lazio would go away. Bergman figures he can cancel the hit on himself by killing the broker and the man who ordered the hit."

"Oh. Wow, I've never heard of that being done, but it would work, wouldn't it?"

"It would if Henry and I weren't involved. Instead, we're going to protect the broker and collect the contract money Bergman is offering."

"You mean you're going to kill the man who offered the contract on Bergman?"

"That's right. And then I'll kill Bergman."

"Hmm."

"What was that 'Hmm' for?"

"When you kill the man who offered the contract on Bergman, you'll be killing your own client. That seems... unethical?"

"He's not my client, because it's an open contract. Had he hired me directly, it would be a different story."

"You're right, and forgive me. I should know that you would never do anything unethical. Assassin or not, you're a man of honor."

"I'll be doing the world a favor. Both men have been involved in human trafficking."

"I know I won't miss them. Give me a few minutes to gather the information and I'll send you everything I have on the brokers."

"Thanks, Crash. I have other people working on this, but the sooner I get to the man, the better the odds are that I can stop him from being killed."

"You're welcome, Tanner. And good luck."

CRASH SENT THE INFORMATION TWELVE MINUTES LATER. A half hour after that, Kate Barlow called and gave Tanner the same information, along with the amount being offered on the contract to kill Lou Lazio. It was a hundred thousand dollars.

To Tanner's surprise, the broker handling the contract on Bergman was someone he knew. The man's name was James Horrigan. During Tanner's years in Las Vegas, Horrigan had worked as a go-between for him, and had once done the same for Spenser.

Their association ended when Horrigan's addiction to cocaine spiraled out of control. However, Tanner had last seen Horrigan years earlier in Colorado. At the time, Horrigan had been clean and had a six-year-old daughter named Beth. Horrigan's ex-wife, Susan, was serving twenty years in prison.

According to the information Crash provided, Jim Horrigan was living in Sarasota, Florida. Tanner knew from information Tim provided that Lou Lazio was in Tucson,

Arizona. Keeping Horrigan alive was vital, but Tanner also wanted to claim the contract on Lazio. When he told Henry that they would protect Horrigan and forget the contract on Lazio, Henry had another suggestion.

"Why not let me fulfill the contract on Lazio while you protect Horrigan?"

"You want to work the contract alone?"

"I can do it. As far as we know, Lazio has no idea he's got a price on his head. He may have a bodyguard or two, but he's not hidden away behind a fortress or on a private island. I'll probably be able to snipe at him from a roof and be on my way in less than a minute."

Tanner sat in a chair that was in front of a rolltop desk and considered Henry's idea. He had decided to take the contract on Bergman to give Henry more experience, and now it had turned into two contracts and the need to protect someone. What was going to be a straightforward hit was turning into a complicated affair. Still, the motivation for taking the contract was to give Henry more practice at his craft while building his confidence in his skills. Taking on a contract alone would do that.

"I think you're ready for Lazio if he isn't heavily guarded."

"Does that mean the contract is mine?"

Tanner locked eyes with him. "I want you to stand down if Lazio has more than two bodyguards."

"I could handle more than that."

"But you won't. Things can go bad fast, Henry. You've received a lot of training, but you're not ready to go out on your own completely. You need more experience, much more."

"And that's why I want this contract. I can do this, Cody."

Tanner was quiet for a moment, then he nodded. "The contract is yours. Head to Tucson but fly into a different city and then drive to where Lazio will be. We'll also have to come up with a legitimate reason for you being there. And I want you to stay in contact."

"I will. When do I leave?"

"As soon as possible. The open contract on Lou Lazio is worth a hundred thousand dollars. You won't be the only one looking to collect it."

"A hundred grand? That's good money."

"And it will all be yours, minus expenses and a ten percent fee to the broker handling it."

"Brokers make ten percent of every contract that passes through their hands? Horrigan must be doing well?"

"He won't be doing anything if I don't reach him in time. I'll be heading to the airport with you; I need to get to Florida."

"What if someone else fulfills the contract on Bergman while we're gone?"

"It won't matter much. We're here to get you experience. You'll be gaining experience by killing Lou Lazio on your own."

"I won't fail."

Tanner smiled at his apprentice. "I know that, Henry. Or else I wouldn't be sending you off alone to Arizona. Lou Lazio doesn't know it yet, but he's a dead man."

4
LONG TIME NO SEE

JIM HORRIGAN WAS ABOUT FIFTY, WAS TALL, AND LOOKED older than he was thanks to his years of being addicted to cocaine and alcohol.

Despite the graying hair and lined face, Tanner thought Horrigan was looking well. He'd put on weight since the last time Tanner had seen him and was in good shape. Tanner caught up to Horrigan while the man was out for a run. Horrigan had covered four miles and did so with ease.

After returning home, Tanner assumed Horrigan would shower. That would be a good time to break into the man's house. The noise of the running water would cover any sounds made while entering.

Someone agreed with Tanner.

Tanner watched a young guy with long hair and tattoos slip over a fence and into Horrigan's backyard. The man's face was familiar. He was one of the guards Tanner had seen from a distance on Bergman's private island. The men guarding Bergman weren't your average rent-a-cops; they were mercenaries who would kill for money. Donahue must have sent the long-haired man to Florida to take care of Horrigan.

The would-be assassin discovered an unlocked window and used it to gain entry to the house. Tanner followed him in and found himself standing inside the bedroom that belonged to Horrigan's daughter. There were posters on the walls of teenaged actors, rock bands, and surprisingly, violinists. There were also a lot of books. Apparently, the girl was a reader.

The guy with the tattoos was easing toward Horrigan's bedroom. There was a connected bathroom, and you could hear a shower running, along with a radio that was playing classic country music. It reminded Tanner that Horrigan had grown up in Colorado.

Tanner attacked the tattooed man while the guy was listening at the bathroom door. He clamped a hand over his mouth and jammed a blade into his chest, to rupture his heart. The guy struggled for two seconds before he went limp. There was little blood other than the massive internal bleeding the wound caused. Tanner dragged the man away from the bathroom door and laid him out on the floor on the far side of the bed. He had died, and if not for the red splotches staining his white shirt, he might have appeared to be asleep.

The shower shut off and was followed a few minutes later by the radio going silent. Jim Horrigan left his bathroom with a towel wrapped around his waist and took four steps to the right to enter a walk-in closet. He had never noticed that Tanner was seated in a chair near the bedroom window.

When he left the closet, Horrigan was zipping up a pair of jeans and carrying a shirt and socks in one hand. He was walking toward the bed when he realized he wasn't alone.

Horrigan said "Shit!" as he became startled and dropped the clothes he was holding. When he realized who it was he was looking at, the rate of his breathing increased, and his hands began shaking.

"Oh God, oh no. Tanner, why are you here? Are you here to kill me?"

"No Jim," Tanner said, then he pointed down at the side of the bed he was on, "but this guy had been sent to kill you."

Horrigan struggled to get his breathing under control. After realizing what Tanner had said, he eased closer and peeked around the bed. When he saw the dead man lying on his bedroom floor, his breathing accelerated again.

"You killed him?"

"I killed him before he could kill you. Alex Bergman wants you dead."

"Alex Bergman? Who is he?"

"He's the target of one of the contracts you're handling, the one worth half a million dollars. He sent this guy here to kill you. Before that happened, you would have been tortured to give up the contract money you're holding."

Horrigan lowered himself into a seated position at the foot of the bed. His bare chest bore the scar of an old gunshot wound. When they'd last seen each other in Colorado, Horrigan had been shot in the chest while saving a young woman from a serial killer. The serial killer had been shot by a cop shortly after, and Horrigan had been named a hero.

"How did Bergman figure out who I was?"

"There are ways. I was told that you're one of only a few people who broker high-value contracts."

Horrigan gazed down at the floor for nearly a minute. When he turned his head to look at Tanner, he seemed to have calmed down.

"Tell me what's going on while I finish getting dressed."

Tanner did so. When he was done, Horrigan said he

hadn't been contacted recently to broker a deal worth a hundred thousand dollars.

"I didn't know Alex Bergman was the target of the half a million-dollar contract. You know that I prefer not to know and usually only pass along the information I receive without reading it. I guess someone else is acting as a middleman on the new contract on Lou Lazio."

"Yeah. And they can expect to pay that out soon. Someone will be killing Lazio today or tomorrow."

"Is that someone you?"

"No. I'll be killing Alex Bergman."

A confused look came over Horrigan. "Half a million is a lot of money, but I've heard that you charge about ten times that these days."

"I normally do, but I've a reason for taking the contract on Bergman. Be glad I did, otherwise you'd be dead."

Horrigan looked at the body on the floor. "We have to do something with him."

"When is your daughter due home?"

"Not until tomorrow. Beth is staying over at a friend's house."

"That's good. We'll wait until most people are asleep and then we'll get rid of the body. You live here; think of a good place to dump him."

"There's nothing better than the ocean, but we'll have to weigh him down."

"You have a boat?"

"I do. Beth loves being out on the water."

"A boat is a good place to hide out. You should live on it until I tell you it's safe to return home. Right now, we'll wrap up the body."

Horrigan held out his hand. "Thank you, Tanner, for saving my life. I owe you one. Hell, I owe you more than one."

Tanner took the offered hand, and they shook. "You had a problem, but it looks like you overcame it."

"I've been clean for a long time, thank God. I never want to go back to the way I was in Las Vegas. Toward the end there, I was a real mess."

"Pack what you'll need for a week, although I doubt you'll have to be on your boat for that long. When I leave Florida, I'll be heading back to Maine to kill Bergman."

"Why does someone want Alex Bergman dead?"

"He spent years abducting women and selling them as sex slaves. They were girls really; they say he specialized in finding girls that were sixteen to nineteen."

Horrigan looked disgusted, then angry. "My daughter is in that age range. That son of a bitch deserves to die."

"So does Lou Lazio. They've put out contracts on each other. And Lazio is as big a dirtbag as Bergman. He'll be dead soon."

"If you're not going to kill him, then who is?"

Tanner smiled. "It's being handled."

HENRY LANDED IN PHOENIX, ARIZONA, AND RENTED A CAR TO make the drive to Tucson. After checking into his hotel room, he drove to the University of Arizona to establish a reason for being in the city. He hated the time it took to create a cover story, but knew it was necessary. And besides, he had an appointment with someone, but that wouldn't take place for three hours. He might as well put the time beforehand to use.

Henry made it a point to be seen wandering around the campus and spoke to the office staff, explaining that he was considering moving to the state and would like to continue his education. It was all a lie, but it was a lie that couldn't be proven. If he later found himself being questioned by the police, he would have a cover story to give them, and it would check out.

Henry found the city to be beautiful and loved the mountainous backdrop. At home in Stark, Texas, most of the land was flat, with here and there a hill. If he were looking to relocate, Tucson would be in the running as a place he might settle.

When the time came for his appointment, Henry drove his rental car to the parking lot of a truck stop out on Route 10 and parked in the back of the lot near a wall. He left his car unlocked and placed a red sheet of paper tucked under a windshield wiper. The red paper was a signal that his was the right car.

After looking around, Henry went inside the truck stop and ordered something to eat. When he came back to his car there was a white van backed up beside it against the wall. It also had a red sheet of paper held in place against its windshield.

Henry opened his car and found a set of keys lying on the seat. They were the keys to the van. After removing the red sheets of paper from the windshields, he shoved them inside the car's glove box and locked up the vehicle.

When he was inside the van, Henry looked behind him and into the cargo area. There was a small crate there that was padlocked. The key for the lock was on the same metal ring that held the van key. Henry started the vehicle to make sure it ran and saw that he had a full tank of gas. The van's motor sounded good, and all the lights worked. He didn't need to be pulled over by a cop for a burnt-out brake light.

He turned off the engine and moved between the seats to enter the cargo area. After opening the crate, he inspected the contents and smiled. There were weapons, including a sniper rifle, along with a bulletproof vest and generation 3 night vision goggles. There were also a variety of ammunition and sound and flash suppressors to go along with the weapons. A small case contained burner phones, lockpicks, and a device useful for disabling alarm systems.

The van and its contents cost twenty-eight thousand dollars. If all but the ammunition and burner phones were returned in good condition, fourteen thousand would be refunded. The contract was for one hundred thousand dollars. After allowing for the broker's ten percent fee, the fourteen thousand spent on the van and weapons, and travel expenses, Henry would clear nearly seventy-five thousand dollars for killing Lou Lazio. Not bad for a day's work. And with Lazio being a first-class scumbag, Henry figured he was making the world a better place.

He activated one of the burner phones that had been provided and sent off a text to Tanner.

All is good. Proceeding as planned—H.

Tanner wrote back to him.

My man is alive and well. Make sure yours isn't—T.

Henry grinned, got behind the wheel of the van, and headed off to kill Lou Lazio.

5
LOVE'S LABOUR'S LOST

L<small>LEWELYN</small> "L<small>OU</small>" L<small>AZIO HAD STARTED OUT IN THE DRUG TRADE</small> as Alex Bergman had also done before getting into human trafficking. As a side business, he'd abducted people and harvested their organs for sale on the black-market. Engaging in such activities had made him a wealthy man, as well as a despicable human being.

You wouldn't know that to look at him. Lazio was handsome, had an athletic build, dressed well, and wore his dark hair long. It gave him a youthful appearance, despite his age of forty-one.

He had recently fallen in love with a young woman of twenty-three who came from a fine family that had roots going back over a hundred years in the Tucson area. Judicious attention to fabricating an identity as a real estate investor had allowed Lazio to retain a reputation as a law-abiding citizen. Few knew that the real estate empire had been funded by his illegal activities. Of those who could prove it, only one was still alive—Alex Bergman.

The young lady who was the subject of Lazio's ardor was Heather Carey. Lazio met the blonde and shapely Heather when he was interested in buying an investment property in Tucson. Heather worked as a real estate agent in the family business and she and Lazio began dating.

Lazio hadn't been in love before and hadn't thought he could feel such emotion; that changed when he met Heather. With his old life behind him and enough money to live in luxury until he died, Lazio began thinking about marriage. Everything would be ruined if his past ever came to light, and so he took steps to prevent that, and at great expense.

Although the contract on Bergman was the most expensive one he had taken out, it had cost him money to have others killed as well. The true price of his actions had yet to be realized by Lazio. By ordering Bergman's death, he had set in motion a string of events that would bring about the end of his own life.

HENRY HAD PICKED UP LAZIO'S TRAIL AT THE ESTATE THE MAN was living in. The former white slaver had recently bought a huge home on the outskirts of Tucson that had a fantastic view of the mountains. Henry considered going in over the wall to find Lazio and hunt him down, but he had been trained to be more cautious than that. There was no hurry, and as yet, he had no idea what defenses or protectors Lazio had.

Tanner had told him to abort the assassination if the man were being guarded by more than two bodyguards. Henry knew he could deal with more than that, but he would do as Tanner asked. He trusted his mentor's opinion and knew that Tanner only had his best interests at heart.

Henry watched the estate through a rifle scope while reclined on a hill. He never spotted Lazio, but there was another man and an older woman in the home. The woman wore an apron and was busy cleaning the living room by dusting and vacuuming; as for the man, he was armed.

The guy had taken off his suit jacket and revealed a shoulder holster. That meant that Lazio had some measure of security protecting him.

When that same man donned a black cap and entered a garage, he came out driving a limousine. Henry understood then that he was a chauffeur as well as a bodyguard.

The limo was pulled around to the side of the house where there was a covered walkway. Henry saw the chauffeur open a rear door for someone and assumed it was Lazio getting into the limo. He saw no one else and the chauffeur rode up front alone.

Henry rushed back to the spot where he'd left the van. He had to get moving or he might lose the limo.

HEATHER CAREY DROVE TOWARD THE TRENDY RESTAURANT IN downtown Tucson with sweaty palms. She was planning to break things off with Lou Lazio.

She'd been infatuated by him in the beginning and had found Lazio to be fascinating, since he had traveled widely and had many stories to tell.

The fact that he was eighteen years her senior hadn't bothered her at first, but over time she realized she wasn't interested in having a long-term relationship with someone so much older. Lazio was only two years younger than her mother, and other than the physical attraction Heather and Lazio felt toward each other, they really had nothing much in common.

Besides, she had recently reconnected with an old high school classmate named Kevin. Heather had a crush on Kevin back then, and she still tingled when she was around him.

Yes, Lou Lazio had been fun, but it was time to end things. She hoped he wouldn't take their break up too hard.

~

LAZIO STARED AT HEATHER WITH AN UNCOMPREHENDING GAZE. He couldn't believe the words she had just uttered. Heather had told him she didn't want to see him anymore. His brain was having trouble accepting that. In his mind, they were to be together forever. Not only that, but he had requested that she join him for dinner in the ridiculously expensive restaurant they were seated in because he planned to ask her to marry him once they had returned to his home.

In his pocket was a diamond ring worth over two hundred thousand dollars. The only way he could have felt more like a fool would be if he had already proposed to her.

"You're serious? You're breaking up with me?"

"Yes, Louis. We had so much fun together, and I'll always be your friend, but I don't think we should see each other again."

"There's someone else, isn't there?"

"I-I never cheated on you, but yes, I've become interested in someone else. He's a boy I went to high school with. We ran into each other, and it just felt... I'm sorry, Louis. I'm sure you'll find someone who's a better match for you."

Lazio kept staring at Heather and really saw her for the first time. She was young, blonde, pretty, and you could find thousands of women in any large city who looked just like her. Why had he ever thought she was something special?

His face was growing red from a mixture of anger and embarrassment. He had bartered and sold women like Heather for over a decade and never gave them anymore consideration than a baker gave to a lump of dough. Women had always been things, pleasant things to screw and valuable things to make money with. How had this one spoiled rich girl gotten under his skin? How had she made him into such a damn fool?

Heather had noticed Lazio's changed demeanor; she reached across the table and touched his arm.

"Louis, are you all right?"

Lazio looked down at his steak knife and imagined what it would feel like to jam it into Heather's lovely throat. His hand twitched toward the knife, but he got ahold of himself.

After taking a deep breath, he spoke in a low voice. "I'm fine, just disappointed, of course."

Heather smiled. "I'm glad you're taking this well; I thought I'd made you angry."

Lazio forced himself to smile back at her. "I'm not angry, honey, just sad."

"Oh, you'll find someone else. There are lots of women who would love to be with you."

"Sure," Lazio said, while keeping the phony smile pasted on his face.

Heather grabbed her purse and stood. "Call me if you ever need real estate advice, you know I'll help you if I can." Heather leaned over and gave him a peck on the cheek. "Goodbye, Louis."

Lazio mumbled goodbye and watched her go. He'd been drinking wine. He signaled to the waiter and when the man came over to the table, Lazio ordered a double whiskey. While he waited for his drink to arrive, he stared at the spot where Heather had sat. She'd known she was breaking up with him and had waited until after the meal to do so. In the meantime, she had ordered lobster and drunk expensive wine.

Lazio laughed, knowing he'd been played like a fool. Heather had used him to have a good time and was moving on to the next man. He'd been an idiot to think she could ever return his love for her.

It was a love that no longer existed. It had been replaced by shame and rage. Someday, he would make her pay for what she'd done. That day wouldn't be soon. If anything bad happened to Heather in the days following their break up, the police would be all over him.

No, he would wait, maybe even for a year or more. But when the time was right, he would make Heather Carey wish she had never been born.

A smile crept onto Lazio's lips. When he did make a move to pay Heather back, he would frame her new boyfriend for her disappearance. It would be a simple matter to find out who the man was, and he would make a great patsy. As for Heather, Lazio would see to it that she suffered before she died.

He left the restaurant after finishing his whiskey and ordered his driver to take him home. He'd had one hell of a shitty day, all he wanted to do was go to sleep and escape it.

HENRY HAD FOLLOWED LAZIO TO THE RESTAURANT AND settled in atop a nearby roof that offered a view inside the expensive eatery. He'd watched Lazio meet with a woman who was young enough to be the man's daughter. He had used the rifle scope to view the couple but had no intention of using the rifle to kill Lazio. It was possible, but too public, and he hadn't worked out a route to use to avoid getting caught. Besides, there was a chance the rifle round would pass through Lazio and kill someone else.

A Tanner never killed the innocent, even inadvertently. As a Tanner in training, Henry was always aware to be careful of causing collateral damage. Lazio was his target and no one else. That included the bodyguard/chauffeur the man had. If possible, Henry would leave the bodyguard alive. An exception would be if the man tried to kill him. Henry didn't think that would happen. He had a plan in mind that would avoid such a confrontation.

Although he hadn't heard the conversation between Lazio and Heather, Henry had interpreted the nature of it.

The guy is being dumped, Henry thought. *Or if it's a first date he struck out badly.*

Either way, it looked like Lazio would be returning home alone. Henry left his position and headed to his van. He needed to beat Lazio back to the estate.

LAZIO ENTERED HIS BEDROOM WHILE CARRYING A BOTTLE. IT was the magnum of champagne he had planned to drink with Heather to celebrate their engagement. Now he had plans to get drunk, but not so drunk that he'd do something stupid. He would pay Heather back someday. In the meantime, he had to act as if her rejection of him was no big deal.

It was a big deal. Beneath the anger and disappointment lay a broken heart. He'd done monstrous things to others, destroyed lives, enslaved and murdered innocents, and never felt any remorse or regret, because those things hadn't happened to him.

To Lazio, other people were like objects, not beings of their own with hearts and souls. Since he was a boy, he'd had no understanding of empathy or compassion. Only he mattered, and only his needs were important. His love for Heather had bordered on need, and the total fulfillment of that desire had been denied him.

He drank until he fell asleep in front of the TV while watching porn. Pornography was more to him than entertainment or titillation; to Lazio, it had always seemed a representation of an ideal way of life. In a porn film, everyone you encountered was there for your pleasure, and women especially existed to serve. No one was in love in a porn movie, all they wanted was to satisfy their lust and basest desires. Life as depicted by pornography was simple, it was a world where no one was ever rejected, and all endings were happy ones.

On the nightstand was the engagement ring he'd bought for Heather. Lazio cursed it as a symbol of his foolishness. When he dreamt, his sleep was filled with images of Heather, and she was laughing at him.

"WAKE UP."

Lazio awoke with a start and released a muffled cry of shock. The cry was muffled because someone wearing a ski mask had a gloved hand clamped over his mouth. That someone was Henry Knight.

Lazio braced himself to sit up in bed then froze as he realized there was the barrel of a gun pressed against his forehead. No, not the barrel, but a sound suppressor that had been screwed onto the barrel.

He stared at Henry and asked a question. The words were unintelligible, and Henry didn't give a damn what he said anyway.

"You're going to die, Lazio. I didn't want you to pass away peacefully in your sleep. I wanted you to see it coming."

Lazio tried to speak louder, and Henry pulled the trigger. Lou Lazio died in a state of great fear. It was but a fraction of a fraction of the terror he had caused his many victims to experience during their abductions and subsequent enslavement.

As he turned to leave, Henry noticed the engagement ring. Lazio must have had plans to ask the woman he'd seen him with to marry him. Instead, she'd broken up with him.

Henry looked down at the dead man. "This really wasn't your day, was it?"

As expected, Lazio didn't answer.

The diamond was huge, and if fenced, would fetch a large price. Henry left the ring where it was. He was an assassin, not a thief. He had completed his work, and now was the time to leave.

Henry departed the estate without setting off an alarm and was back at his hotel before midnight. When a bored desk clerk asked him how his night had gone, Henry smiled at him.

"It was uneventful."

6
ASK, AND YE SHALL RECEIVE

Horrigan's boat was a Sundancer 320. He had named it after his daughter; it was called the *Beth Anne*. It was after two a.m. when they carried the dead man's body onto the boat inside a huge ice chest. The bottom of the chest had holes drilled into it, while the top of the chest had been sealed shut with the use of a waterproof epoxy that should keep it closed for a good long time. When the seal finally broke and the lid on the chest popped open, the body inside the ice chest would be no more than bones.

Tanner instructed Horrigan to take them out of Sarasota Bay and into the Gulf of Mexico. Given the late hour and the darkness, there was little chance they would be seen by anyone.

Horrigan had calmed down and had thanked Tanner again for saving his life. They had talked about their days in Las Vegas together over a dinner of pizza and beer, and then Horrigan went on to brag about his daughter, who was a prodigy with the violin.

Tanner listened and nodded but offered no information about his own life. He'd been a loner when Horrigan knew him, and the man likely assumed that was still the case. Horrigan would have been shocked to learn that Tanner was happily married and the father of two children. Tanner was shocked by his life as well. It wasn't that long ago he thought he would never marry and would die alone. Now he had a family, had regained his true identity of Cody Parker, and was back living on the land where he had grown up. At times, it seemed a miracle to him.

They navigated through the bay and moved out onto the Gulf. The sea was calm and the sky clear, giving a spectacular view of the stars. Tanner decided it might be a good idea to rent a boat someday soon and have a vacation on the water with Sara and the children. His cousin, Mr. White, owned a vacation home down in the Keys and had invited them to visit. Tanner figured he'd take White up on that offer soon.

After heading due west for five nautical miles, Horrigan asked Tanner if he thought they were out far enough. Tanner told him to keep going for a little longer. When they had traveled farther from land, Tanner judged that they had reached their destination.

The ice cooler was dumped overboard without ceremony or consideration of the dead man within it. If his Maine driver's license was real, the man had been one Jay Collins and he had been twenty-eight. He'd come to Florida to take a life while playing at being an assassin and had lost his own life at the hands of the greatest assassin who had ever lived.

Tanner and Horrigan watched the ice chest slip below the surface before heading back to Sarasota. After Horrigan dropped Tanner off at the marina, they would still have work to do. The dead man, Jay Collins, had driven a rented vehicle to Horrigan's house. That car had to be left somewhere that wouldn't link it to Horrigan, although a search of the vehicle's navigation records would reveal that it had been parked in Horrigan's neighborhood. Jay Collins had not parked it in front of Horrigan's home, but across the street and several doors down.

Tanner had already driven the vehicle to an area near the dock, but now it was time to get rid of it. As Tanner drove Collins' rental, he followed directions Horrigan had given him. Those directions took him into an area where the crime rate was high. He left the rental car unlocked and with the key fob in plain view on the dashboard, with the hope that it would be stolen and wind up at a chop shop.

Horrigan was waiting for him several blocks away on a main drag. Had he followed Tanner any closer it might have left a record of his being in the same area where Collins' car had been.

Tanner detected the footfalls behind him as he strode down an unlit street. When they were joined by another set of feet, he figured he had attracted trouble. That was not uncommon. Trouble had a way of following him around.

When the footfalls quickened, a voice called out. "Yo! My man, wait up."

Tanner turned and saw two men headed his way. One was white and the other was Hispanic. They were dressed in layers despite the warmth in the air. It made them appear bigger and the layers could act as padding against blows if a potential victim fought back. The white man was holding a long knife; his friend was gripping a baseball bat. It had been the Hispanic man who had spoken; he did so again as they closed in on Tanner.

"Give us your shit or we'll fuck you up."

Tanner said, "All right," and took out his gun. The two men froze in place long enough for Tanner to have time to screw a sound suppressor onto the end of it. He shot the white man in the face and the Hispanic man took a round to the back of his head, as the guy turned to flee.

The bodies, along with the bat and the knife, fell to the

ground and made more noise than the two shots had. Tanner continued walking until he reached a wide street where Horrigan was waiting for him.

"I'd be willing to bet that car will be stolen before the sun comes up," Horrigan said. "This area is full of thieves and muggers."

"I met two of them on my walk back here."

"You did? What happened?"

"They said they would hurt me if I didn't give them something, so I gave them each a bullet."

"They're dead?"

"They're dead."

Horrigan stared at Tanner. The man had been in Sarasota for only a few hours and three men were dead. If he hadn't come to town, Horrigan knew he would have died instead.

"If you ever need a favor from me, Tanner, just ask."

"All I need you to do right now is to get on that boat of yours for a few days. I'll let you know when it's safe to return home."

As they drove back toward the marina, Tanner received a text from Henry. It was short and to the point.

One down. One to go.

Tanner knew that meant that Lou Lazio was dead. Henry had traveled across the country and carried out an assassination on his own. He looked forward to hearing the details when they were together again in Maine.

One man was down, and Alex Bergman was next. His guards and his secluded island retreat wouldn't be enough to save him.

Tanner watched Horrigan head out on his boat before driving off to find a hotel to spend the night in. After changing his mind, he took out his phone and checked available flights to Maine. When he learned it was possible to charter a jet that could leave at six a.m., he decided to head to the airport instead. There would be plenty of time to sleep during the flight, and he wanted to get back to Maine as soon as possible.

Alex Bergman wasn't the toughest target he had ever taken on, but Tanner didn't assume that killing the man would be easy, and he had yet to come up with a plan. He decided that more surveillance was needed, and that more information had to be gathered.

And when the time was right, Alex Bergman would die.

7
GOOD NEWS, BAD NEWS

B<small>ERGMAN</small> <small>PUMPED</small> <small>A</small> <small>FIST</small> <small>INTO</small> <small>THE</small> <small>AIR</small> <small>WHEN</small> <small>HE</small> <small>LEARNED</small> that Lou Lazio was dead. His elation faded rapidly when Donahue delivered his next bit of news.

"The man I sent to kill the broker, Horrigan, isn't answering his phone. I think we have to assume the worst."

"Meaning what?"

"Our man is dead, and Horrigan is still alive. As long as he's alive, the contract Lazio put out on you is still active."

"Even though Lazio is dead?"

"Lou Lazio is dead, but his money, the half a million, is still there waiting to be claimed by anyone that kills you."

"Damn it!"

"I know. But Alex, Horrigan can't stay hidden forever. And after a while he'll realize keeping the contract active isn't worth the risk."

"And until then what? I have to stay hidden here?"

"You do if you want to keep living."

Bergman's fingers curled into claws, and he brought his hands together as if he were strangling someone.

"Damn Lou Lazio to hell. Not only did that bastard cost

me a hundred thousand dollars to get rid of him, but paying for all these damn guards and security measures is eating up my money as well. Mike, isn't there something else we can do?"

"I've got private investigators searching for Horrigan. They've already uncovered the fact that the man has a daughter. If we locate her and kidnap her, he'll be forced to do as we say."

"Yes. That could work."

Donahue raised up a hand. "Don't get your hopes up. My guess is that Horrigan has the girl with him, wherever he is. If so, we'll have nothing to use against him."

Bergman's shoulders slumped. "Someone is going to try to kill me again soon. That half a million dollars will bring hit men out of the woodwork."

"Well, there's one thing to be grateful for."

"What's that?"

"I don't think it's enough money to attract the best, like Tanner. If he took the contract, you might as well kill yourself and be done with it."

"Thank God for small favors," Bergman said. If he'd known that Tanner was nearby, his despair would have tripled.

TANNER HAD DECIDED HE NEEDED TO KNOW MORE ABOUT Driftwood Island and its defenses before he set foot upon it. To accomplish that, he was going to move around the perimeter of the island while wearing scuba gear. Bergman's retreat took up nineteen acres. It would take great effort to circumnavigate it while swimming underwater for most of the time.

Henry would be nearby in a boat and carrying a rifle if

Tanner needed someone to create a diversion, were the guards to detect him. Tanner didn't think that would be necessary, as he had no plans to go ashore. However, that might be his next step before committing to an assassination attempt.

Henry had given Tanner the details about his killing of Lou Lazio. Tanner was pleased to learn that Henry had taken precautions before entering Lou Lazio's home. Those precautions, or due diligence, as Tanner's own mentor, Spenser, like to call them, could wind up being either a waste of time, or the difference between life and death.

Henry's due diligence had wound up being unneeded, and his hit on Lou Lazio had been flawless. Anyone investigating the crime would have no way to tie the death to Henry. They would be forced to conclude that Lou Lazio had been murdered by an unknown professional killer.

"Were you tempted to take the engagement ring you told me about?" Tanner asked, as they sat together inside the rented home.

"Only for a moment. But I wasn't there to rob the man, I was there to kill him."

"That's right. And had you tried to fence that ring, it might have led the cops to your doorstep someday. Now, if that had been a pile of cash, there would have been no reason you couldn't have taken it."

"Did you ever steal anything from the site of a hit that wasn't cash?"

"Yeah, I did. But I never had a permanent address back then, and I wasn't living under my real name. If a cop tried to track me down, it would have been like chasing a ghost."

They left the house and went off to acquire scuba gear. As a precaution, Tanner drove an hour away up the coast to buy what he wanted. The shop was near a beach, one that had few people around. Tanner decided he needed to practice; it had been quite a while since he'd gone scuba diving and he wanted to make sure there were no problems with his equipment.

The equipment performed well, and he did just as well while swimming underwater. He had no doubt he would be sore for a few days after the unusual exertion of swimming around the island, but he was in excellent condition and his body would recover quickly.

By the time they left the beach, Tanner was confident he was ready to learn more about Bergman's defenses by using the scuba gear.

He and Henry stopped for dinner on the way back, and as they sat waiting for their dessert to be served, Tanner received a call from Tim Jackson.

"You have news, Tim?"

"Yeah, but I don't know if it will help you any."

"What is it?"

"Donahue made a call to someone and ordered prostitutes, ten of them. Two of them will be for him and Bergman, the rest are for the guards. There will be a boat bringing them to the island around seven o'clock, then they'll pick them up in the morning."

"That could be useful. If nothing else, the guards will be distracted, along with Donahue and Bergman."

"Are you making your move tonight?"

"No. Not until I know more about the layout of the island, which I plan to do tonight. Thanks, Tim. Is there anything else?"

"Donahue received a call from someone saying they couldn't find *the girl*, but they never said the girl's name. Does that mean anything to you?"

"It does. It means that Horrigan and his daughter are safe."

"Oh, right, Bergman wanted to kidnap Horrigan's daughter and use her against him."

"Yeah. If they had gotten her, Horrigan would have done anything to make sure she stayed safe, even given himself up to be killed."

"Bergman really is a bastard. I'll let you know if I learn anything else."

"Do that. And thanks again."

They left the restaurant and returned to the rented house, where they waited for it to get dark. By nine o'clock, Tanner was in the water and moving along the island's shoreline. When he heard gunshots, he wondered if someone else had claimed the contract on Alex Bergman.

8
ECHO

ALEX BERGMAN HAD ORDERED TEN HOOKERS, BUT ELEVEN women had shown up on the island. One of them was an aspiring assassin going by the name of Echo. She was a blonde beauty with a figure as good as any of the women hired to provide pleasure. She brought along a pair of skimpy red shorts and a matching halter top to fit in with the others.

Echo hadn't arrived by boat, although she had used a small boat to reach the area. Afterward, she had swum to Driftwood Island in a one-piece green bathing suit while using flippers and a snorkel. She was young and in shape and had assumed reaching the island would be no big deal since she could make frequent stops for rest on some of the smaller islands in the area. She'd been wrong. Even with the breaks, the swim had taken everything she had, and the water had been so cold that her teeth had chattered.

Fortunately, she had arrived on the island early and had time to recover her strength. She did so after climbing up a tree where she could observe the house. Her weapons consisted of a small gun and the element of surprise. She reasoned that Bergman would take her for one of the hookers and allow her to get close to him. Close enough to kiss, near enough to kill.

Echo had fulfilled six open contracts since becoming an assassin a year earlier. So far, a thirty-thousand-dollar payday had been the most she'd earned. Going after Bergman was out of her league, she knew, but she also assumed that the way to change leagues was to push yourself to exceed your limits. If she could kill Bergman, a man guarded by over twenty defenders and living on an island, she would know she was ready to take on greater challenges.

Unlike Bergman, Echo would be thrilled to learn that Tanner was nearby. She wanted nothing more than to be like the man, had been inspired to become an assassin because of him, and she had met him once, long ago, when Tanner had saved her and her mother.

Echo had left the tree as night was falling and moved with caution toward a building she had identified as the mess hall. In actuality, it was a large storage shed. Bergman had converted it into a dining hall for the guards; it was where they took their meals.

A catering service on the mainland prepared food that was picked up every ten days. Those meals were then stored in freezers to be heated up later and were eaten for dinner. The guards fended for themselves the rest of the time and were allowed to drink beer during their off-hours. Outside the shed was a propane-powered grill, and inside were two refrigerators crammed with eggs, cold cuts, and fruit. There was also an abundant supply of fresh fish to be had from the surrounding sea.

Echo was starving. The swimming had exhausted her, and after sitting up a tree for hours she was famished and thirsty.

I would have brought food along if I had planned better, she admonished herself.

Her inability to account for how tiring the swim would be had made her doubt her chances at succeeding. For a moment, she considered leaving the island as soon as she could. If she stayed and made a serious mistake, one of Bergman's guards would kill her.

No, she told herself. *There's no quitting. This is do or die.*

Echo found cold cuts, bread, and mustard in the mess hall. She made a sandwich and wolfed it down between gulps from a can of soda. As she ate, she kept watch by peeking out the corner of a window and saw one of the patrolling guards walk by near the shore holding a rifle. The man was barely visible in the moonlight, but he'd been using a flashlight.

If the guard was looking for a sign that someone had come ashore, he wouldn't find any, or so she hoped. Echo had arrived during high tide and most of her footprints had been washed away by the waves. When she'd reached an expanse of dry ground, she had lowered herself onto her side and rolled along in the sand until she touched a grassy area. The guard might notice an odd pattern in the sand, but he wouldn't see footprints.

When the guard paused at the spot where she had rolled around, Echo held her breath. When he headed for the trees, she wondered if he was following her trail. If so, he might stumble upon the spot where she'd hidden her snorkel and flippers.

That didn't happen. The man wasn't following her trail. He had only stepped into the trees to take a leak. Echo saw the man make a motion like he was pulling down a zipper and realized what he was doing. Her relief was short-lived, because the voices of two men came from nearby and were getting louder.

Along with the twin refrigerators, the dining hall had a

large cabinet that was being used as a pantry. Echo stepped inside the cabinet and backed into the space between the shelves. She managed to shut the door a moment before the men entered the dining hall.

She eased her gun out as their voices grew nearer. The voices moved past the pantry, and she heard a refrigerator open. The men seemed to be in a good mood and were talking about the hookers that were expected to arrive soon.

Echo heard the popping sound made when someone opened a can of beer, then the sound came again, as the second man opened his can. The men exited the dining hall a few moments later and Echo decided she should do the same.

She was startled when an airhorn sounded off, but then she smiled. That was the signal that the boat with the hookers was arriving. Echo stayed to the shadows and eased her way toward the house where Alex Bergman lived. She was determined to make it the home he died in.

BERGMAN HAD LISTENED TO DONAHUE TELL HIM HOW RISKY IT was to bring anyone to the island, then he told him to hire the hookers anyway. His stress level was high, and sex was a great way to relax. Besides, the guards were going as stir crazy as he was being cooped up on the island day after day. A night of sex would do everyone some good, and the guards would appreciate the gesture. Bergman wanted the guards to like him. If they didn't like him, one of them might decide to kill him and claim the price he had on his head.

Despite Donahue's protestations, Bergman noticed that he had ordered a woman for himself. As usual, she was a tall blonde. Donahue had a thing for tall blondes. Bergman didn't care what height a woman was if she was good-looking. The woman he'd picked out was beautiful and had skin the color of cocoa butter, with eyes as blue as the sky. As he took her in his arms, Bergman felt his tension slipping away.

ECHO SMILED SEDUCTIVELY AT THE MAN STANDING GUARD outside Alex Bergman's bedroom door. He was about forty and had a beard. She had neglected to pack food, but she had brought along a disguise of sorts in a watertight bag. Her face was caked in makeup, and she wore a long black wig that cascaded down her back. She thought she looked like a clown, but the guard was giving her an appreciative stare. Of course, his eyes were focused on her breasts, which were all but spilling out of the tiny halter top she wore.

"I was sent up here to party with your boss."

"And what a lucky bastard he is. I get off work in three hours. If you're finished with the boss by then, come and find me. My name is Nate."

Echo looked him up and down. "I'll do that. For now, how about a preview of things to come?" Echo moved closer and raised her arms, to wrap them around the guard's neck. The guard, Nate, leaned in for a kiss only to jerk his head up when he felt the sharp pinch at the base of his neck. Echo had injected him with a drug that would knock him out. The drug was a derivative of propofol that had been mixed with other sedatives. Echo had acquired it on the black-market along with the large ring she wore. The ring could be used as a needle to inject the drug. It had a single use. Echo thought it was like something from a spy movie and wouldn't work. Then she'd seen it used on someone by the guy she'd bought it from. The victim had been a homeless man, and the drug had knocked him out within seconds. Echo had left behind a hundred bucks to make it up to the man, even though she hadn't been the one to drug him.

The guard, Nate, opened his mouth to speak at the same time his eyes closed on their own. He tried to fight it, but the drug was too powerful. He could no longer stand within five seconds of receiving the drug and collapsed.

Echo winced at the sound the guard's body made as it hit the floor. She had brought along the drug to avoid making noise with a gun, but the guard's own weapon, his rifle, made a loud clunking sound as it struck the hardwood floor outside Bergman's bedroom.

Echo supposed it didn't matter much, as there was a possibility that someone was watching them with the use of a hidden camera. If so, she'd been seen drugging Nate. The best thing she could do was to keep moving and kill Bergman as quickly as possible. After that, she would have to run for her life to make an escape.

She entered the bedroom to receive her next bit of bad luck. Bergman wasn't alone. He was with a woman and the two of them were naked and were tangled in an embrace on the bed.

"Two is better than one," Echo said with a smile, and headed toward them.

Bergman smiled back at her. "Get over here and get naked."

Echo raised her left hand up to her neck as she drew closer to Bergman. Her gun was taped in place at the top of her back and hidden from view beneath the dark wig. Another few steps and she'd put a bullet right between Bergman's eyes. He didn't suspect a thing and believed she was another one of the hookers.

The real hooker knew that wasn't true. She pointed at Echo. "Who are you?"

Bergman raised himself to his knees in a rush. "You don't recognize her?"

"I've never seen her before," the hooker said.

Echo had freed the gun. By the time she had it pointed at Bergman, he had grabbed the hooker by her hair and was using her as a human shield. Echo cursed and moved the gun around to get a clear shot. She could kill them both, but the woman was an innocent as far as Echo was concerned. She didn't kill indiscriminately.

The hooker was screaming with the gun pointed at her and struggling to get free. Bergman held her hair with his right hand, while his left hand opened a drawer on the nightstand. When his hand came out holding a gun, Echo dived to the floor at the foot of the bed.

Bergman released the hooker, and she went screaming out of the room.

Knowing she had to get away in the next few seconds or be killed, Echo rose from the floor while firing at the bed, assuming Bergman was still on it. She was half right, as he had one foot on the floor and the other still on the bed. Her hurried shot had missed and splintered the wooden headboard behind him. Bergman returned fire and the glass on the patio doors shattered. Echo fired again only to miss as Bergman dove to the floor. She turned and fled through a gap in one of the patio doors, where the glass had been. One of the remaining shards cut a line of red across her shoulder as she passed through.

Bergman fired at her again as she leapt from the marble balcony and into the swimming pool below. The coolness of the water shocked her, and her wig became heavy with the weight of the liquid clinging to it. Echo ripped the wig from her head before scrambling from the pool, then heard a bullet whiz past her right ear.

Bergman was on the balcony and firing down at her. She

would have loved to fire back, but her gun was at the bottom of the pool, having left her hand when she'd impacted with the water. She'd also lost one of the sandals she'd been wearing. Echo rushed into the trees with one shoe on as a siren went off and lights blazed on to full brilliance. The shouts of men came from all around as the guards began their search for her.

She knew she'd never make it back to the spot where she'd left her snorkel and flippers without being seen, so she headed straight for the beach. If she could make it into the surf, she might have a chance at surviving.

She grunted in pain as she passed a thorny bush that scraped her exposed midsection. Then let out a short scream as a line of bullets tore into the trees less than a yard to her left. She began weaving to make her route less predictable and more bullets passed through the area she would have been at had she kept going straight.

She flung the remaining sandal from her foot to move faster. Finally, she reached the edge of the trees and spotted the water. As she cut across the sand a Jeep appeared on her right. Fortunately, it was far down the beach and wouldn't reach her before she made it into the water. Unfortunately, someone in the Jeep had a rifle. The vehicle came to a hard stop and the rifleman took careful aim.

Echo made it into the water and was diving into the waves when she heard the shot and felt the explosion of pain in her right thigh. She'd barely made the daytime swim to the island with the aid of a snorkel and fins and frequent breaks. Wounded and weary, and with diminishing strength, Echo wondered if she would die by drowning. She swam as fast as she could as the pain in her leg increased. She had been unsuccessful at killing Bergman, and that failure might be paid for with her life.

9

AIR TO SPARE

THE GUNSHOTS TANNER HEARD HAD BEEN MADE BY THE
guards as they chased Echo. He had been too far away to
hear the shots taken during the brief firefight inside
Bergman's bedroom.

He was in his scuba gear with his head above the water's
surface, as he tried to discern where the shots were coming
from. To his left and fifty yards away on the beach, a man
standing up in a Jeep took a shot at someone. A pickup truck
appeared from the opposite direction and the two vehicles
converged on a spot that was halfway between them.
Whoever had been shot at had made it into the surf. The rifle
barked again as the man holding it fired into the water, likely
hoping to get lucky and hit his fleeing target.

When the vehicles drove off toward the dock, Tanner
submerged himself and went looking for their quarry.

DONAHUE HAD BEEN THE MAN WITH THE RIFLE. HE WAS
certain he had hit Echo at least once. He and the men in the

other vehicle drove to the dock and climbed aboard a pair of boats with powerful outboard motors. They were going to hunt down Echo to bring her back alive or recover her corpse if possible. If she was alive, she wouldn't stay that way for long.

Bergman had told him that the failed assassin had been a woman. His first thought had been that one of the hookers must have learned of the price on Bergman's head and tried to cash in. But no, all ten hookers had been accounted for. Donahue had been with one of them when the alarm went off inside the house. That was something else he owed the assassin, as he'd yet to have sex with the hooker he'd chosen.

Donahue shouted instructions to the men who would drive the boats. He wanted them to go back and forth in a definite pattern as they searched for the woman.

"She's wounded. She won't have the strength to make it to the nearest island. There's a thousand-dollar bonus to the man that spots her."

The other men grinned, and the sea hunt began.

I'M NOT GOING TO MAKE IT, ECHO THOUGHT, AS SHE FLOATED on her back and sucked in air. Overhead was a panorama of brilliant stars, they were unconcerned over her fate, as was the water beneath her.

After moving out some distance from Driftwood Island, she swam below the surface, assuming that she would be fired upon if spotted. Unable to hold her breath any longer, she surfaced and swam some more, then paused to rest. The water seemed colder than earlier and wasn't as calm as it had been, although it was far from being choppy.

When she looked back at the island, she was surprised that it was still close. A look in the other direction revealed the dark outline of the nearest island. That small mass of land looked to be so very far away, impossibly far, and Echo's wounded leg was ablaze with pain.

She began swimming again, knowing that time wasn't her friend. She had to keep moving before she grew too weak to swim and drowned. Being captured became a greater fear than drowning when she heard boat motors and looked over her shoulder to see searchlights. She could imagine what fate would befall her if Bergman got his hands on her.

A voice cried out, "I see her!" and Echo dove beneath the surface once more.

DONAHUE AND THE MEN IN THE OTHER BOAT TURNED THEIR searchlights toward the area one of the men had pointed to. Donahue saw a frightened face take in a gulp of air an instant before that face submerged. There was something else as well, a trace of red was mixed in with the water. Their prey was wounded.

One of the men took aim at the spot with a rifle, but Donahue ordered everyone to hold their fire.

"We don't need to shoot her; she can only hold her breath for so long, and then we'll have her."

TANNER WAS BELOW THE SURFACE OF THE WATER NEAR THE spot where Echo had been seen. He had lost sight of her, but thanks to the glow given off by the searchlights he knew she must be nearby. There was moonlight above, but all he had to see by was the light given off by the headlamp he wore. When a shape drifted past the beam of his light, he saw long blonde hair and a shapely figure. Until then, he'd assumed the swimmer was a man. The woman became aware of him, and an alarmed expression made her eyes go wide. She must have assumed he was one of Bergman's men looking to capture her. She headed for the surface with Tanner in pursuit.

∿

DONAHUE HEARD A LOUD GASP COME FROM SOMEWHERE behind him and turned his searchlight toward the sound. The light revealed Echo's open mouth as she sucked in air. Donahue called to her.

"You can't get away! And I know you're wounded. If you keep diving like that, sooner or later you won't make it back up. Swim over here and let us help you."

∿

ECHO WAS TOO BUSY TREADING WATER AND GULPING IN AIR TO respond to Donahue verbally, so she raised her left hand and gave him the finger. She'd rather drown than be at the mercy of him and the men with him. And anyway, she had a plan. She had run from the scuba diver she saw, but now she would seek him out. She still had a small blade on her. If she could kill the scuba diver, she could take his gear and make it to safety. It was a long shot, but it was also a chance to survive. Echo took in a final breath and dove under the water again.

∿

TANNER SAW ECHO HEADED FOR HIM. THE STARTLED expression that had been on her face moments earlier had been replaced by a look of determination. But her expressions were nearly made comical by the makeup smeared across her face. When he saw the blade gripped in her left hand, he knew what she had planned.

He let her come to him, let her make her move, then gripped the wrist that was connected to the hand holding the knife. Echo's face contorted in pain, and she nearly opened her mouth, as Tanner squeezed her wrist hard. She tried to hit him, but her free hand was batted away, then the knife was pried loose from her fingers and drifted toward the bottom of the ocean.

Tanner brought his legs up and wrapped them around her waist, trapping her, then he pulled something free from the harness holding his air tank and thrust it at Echo's face.

ECHO WAS NEAR PANIC KNOWING SHE COULDN'T BREAK Tanner's grip and thinking he meant to hold onto her until she drowned. That wouldn't take long; she was running out of air. When he shoved the object at her face, she thought it was a weapon of some kind and jerked her head away. He forced it to her mouth, and she saw writing on the side of the cylindrical object that was illuminated by the headlamp he wore. There were two words written in black lettering on a yellow background: SPARE AIR.

Tanner was trying to give her air from one of those emergency mini scuba tanks divers carried. Echo had carried one a year earlier when she and a former boyfriend had gone diving in the Bahamas. She calmed down and accepted the gift, then put it to use. Without it, she would have died, as her lungs had reached their breaking point. It was then that she knew Tanner wasn't with Bergman's people, and she wondered who he was and why he was scuba diving near the island at night.

Tanner nodded when she accepted the gift of life. The details of his face were lost in the glare coming off his headlamp, but Echo had made out the motion of his nod. He then pointed toward the nearest island and began tugging her in that direction. Echo made her own nodding motion and began swimming. The ache in her right leg was bad and getting worse; her strength was nearing its end. Echo kept swimming, knowing she had no choice. It was either keep swimming or die.

～

BY DONAHUE'S ESTIMATE, THEY HADN'T SEEN THE GIRL FOR nearly four minutes. He was certain they would have spotted her or heard her if she had surfaced nearby to gulp in air. Perhaps she had drowned. Unwilling to count on that he ordered the men with him to head for the nearest island, where they would search for her.

"The bitch probably drowned by now, but if not, maybe we'll get lucky and find her on shore. Wounded the way she is, she wouldn't get far."

The man who had first spotted Echo pointed to their left and behind them. "I hear another motor."

Donahue heard it too but saw nothing. Whoever was out there was running dark. Several of the men pointed their flashlights toward the new arrival. It was a boat like the ones they were in. It had slowed and was circling them.

"I thought we only had two boats."

"We do only have two boats," Donahue said. As the words were leaving his mouth, he spotted the outline of a rifle. It was being held by someone crouched low at the side of the boat. Before he could issue a warning to the others, he heard the shots. It was the boom of high caliber rounds being fired.

Donahue dropped to the deck, then realized he and the

others weren't the intended targets. The boat's motors had been hit, along with the motors on the other boat. Someone had been very lucky with their shots, or they were equipped with night vision and were proficient with a rifle. Their skill was even more impressive given that they were firing from a moving boat.

The man who'd first heard the boat raised his own rifle to his shoulder to return fire. By then, the other boat was in darkness again, as the men who had been pointing their flashlights at it were keeping low. Donahue shouted for his man to get down, but his warning was too late. The man was hit in the chest and a chunk of his torso went missing amidst a spray of blood. The body fell overboard and into the water.

"Everybody stay down! The man must have night vision."

The unseen boat's motors revved up and could be heard to speed away. Donahue didn't raise his head until the sound was no more than a distant hum. The woman assassin must have had a partner. If so, there might be another attempt made on Bergman's life, and soon. Donahue used his searchlight as he attempted to locate the body of the slain guard but saw nothing but blood on the water. The body had sunk beneath the surface.

There was a satellite phone aboard the boat. Donahue found it and called the island to give Bergman the bad news.

THE MINI SCUBA TANK HAD RUN OUT OF AIR AND ECHO HAD run out of energy. Tanner guided her along as she floated on her back and could feel her shiver. She let out a cry of distress when a boat approached. Tanner paused to look and saw a light flashing the signal he and Henry had agreed on.

"It's okay," Tanner told Echo. "That's a friend coming to give us a lift back to the mainland."

Echo said nothing but seemed to relax, although her shivering increased. It was no wonder she was cold. Tanner was chilled and he was wearing a wet suit designed to help him keep warm. Tanner turned his headlamp on and off in a pattern to signal Henry, then he waited for the boat to pull up beside them. When he felt Echo go limp, he realized she had passed out, possibly from blood loss.

Henry pulled Echo aboard first. His surprise at seeing her was evident. Some of his surprise came from the fact that Echo's breasts were exposed. The scanty halter top she'd been wearing had come loose in the water. After settling her on a padded bench, Henry draped a blanket over her.

"I see you picked up a hitchhiker," he said, as he helped Tanner into the boat.

"Yeah, she was the one being chased, not me. I never made it to the island."

"No one is chasing her now. I disabled their motors and killed a fool who tried to shoot back."

"Good man."

Tanner had taken off his scuba diving equipment, including the mask. Echo had regained consciousness; when she saw Tanner's face, she pointed up at him, said, "It's you," and then passed out again.

"Do you know her?" Henry asked.

"She doesn't look familiar. And she needs medical care. Take us in while I try to stop that leg wound from bleeding."

"Do you think she killed Bergman?"

"Maybe. I guess we'll find out when she comes to."

"Whoever she is, she's got guts."

"And luck. If we hadn't been here, she'd be dead."

Henry headed toward the mainland and back to the private boathouse where the vessel would be stored. Tanner had ventured toward the island to gather information, and now had only more questions. He stared down at Echo and wondered who she was, then he grabbed the first aid kit and went to work on her leg wound.

Whoever she was, she had just made killing Bergman more difficult. If the man still lived, he would likely increase his security, or perhaps flee the island and hide somewhere else. What had been a difficult assassination may have just become more challenging.

Echo moaned as Tanner cleaned her wound to examine it, but her eyes never opened. Whether she had managed to kill Bergman or not, she'd gone to the island, and possibly all alone.

Tanner decided Henry was right, the woman had guts.

The boat chugged on as the land grew nearer on a moonlit night in Maine.

10
WELCOME TO THE CLUB

B ERGMAN'S CLOSE CALL OF THE PREVIOUS NIGHT HAD RATTLED him so much that he never did have sex with the hooker he'd been with. He'd been naked and in an aroused state when Echo had entered his bedroom. His degree of lust—among other things—had deflated rapidly once he'd had a loaded gun pointed toward him.

Donahue's call telling him that a guard had been killed by the woman's partner hadn't done anything to place him at ease and he'd been up all night thinking about the situation.

That thinking took place in a guest room, since his bedroom was no longer safe. The glass on the patio doors had been shattered during the shoot-out and there was nothing to prevent an intruder or the cool night air from entering. A guard had been stationed in the room until the glass could be replaced, and security upgraded.

Perhaps the wounded woman had drowned, but there was still the unknown partner to be considered. Would that person think themselves lucky to have gotten away, or would they be enraged by the loss of the woman and be looking for revenge?

Even if Horrigan was located and the contract was cancelled, that person might still want to kill him, Bergman reasoned. To prevent that, he was going to spend yet more money to try to find whoever had killed the guard. Along with that, he decided to increase his security. When he informed Donahue of his decision while meeting in the room he was temporarily using, his friend had a suggestion.

"Keep the new guards on a nearby island."

Bergman stopped pacing and stared at his friend. "What good will that do?"

"They might be able to stop an attack before it happens, since anyone traveling here will likely approach from the mainland and have to navigate around the other islands. Also, if we supply them with boats and there is another attack, they can respond, and we'll have the attackers in a kind of pincer movement. If we'd had people on the nearest island yesterday, there's a chance they might have spotted the girl and her partner as they were headed here."

Bergman nodded after considering the idea. "It makes sense. How many more men do you think we'll need?"

"At least eight, with two more boats. We need night vision equipment too. If I'd had it last night, I could have fired back at the man who shot at us."

"Are you sure it was a man?"

Donahue shrugged. "No, it's just a guess."

"More men, more boats, and night vision equipment. If this keeps up, I'm going to have to get back into business or go broke."

Donahue reached out and patted his friend's shoulder. "This will end soon, Alex. I'll make sure of it."

Bergman released a heavy sigh. "All right. If I'm going to do this, I'm going all out. Hire twelve more guards, give them all the gear they need, and upgrade the equipment here."

"That's a good idea. The patio doors in your bedroom are

getting bulletproof glass and so are the windows, along with a new alarm system, entry door, and electronic locks. It won't be cheap, but you'll be safer."

Bergman held up a hand. "One more thing."

"Yeah?"

"Hire whoever you need to, but I want Horrigan located. If the contract goes away, so do most of my problems. And find that bitch who shot at me last night."

"I think she's dead."

"Her partner isn't dead. If you can't find the girl, then find whoever was helping her. I won't be safe until you do."

"I'll make it happen. Until then, there will always be three guards here. One will be outside your door, while the other two stand guard in front of the home."

Bergman settled heavily into a chair. "I always feared I'd wind up in a prison cell someday. I might as well be in one now with the lack of freedom I have here."

Donahue headed for the door. "I'll get started on making these changes; the first thing I'll do is hire more guards."

"What about the man who was killed on the boat last night, has his body washed up on shore?"

"No. One of the other guards grew up in the area and does a lot of fishing. He thinks the body probably washed out to sea, or else it will wind up here like all the driftwood does."

"That's one blessing. If his body was found, we might have to deal with cops looking into it."

Donahue opened the door, then turned back to look at Bergman. "Alex."

"Yeah."

"Keep a gun handy at all times, just in case."

Bergman lifted his shirt and revealed the gun he had tucked in his waistband. "I'm way ahead of you."

TANNER HAD DONE WHAT HE COULD TO TREAT ECHO'S WOUNDS before deciding she needed a doctor. After making a call to Joe Pullo, Tanner was given an address where he would find a doctor that asked no questions. He and Henry loaded Echo into the van and arrived at a home that was a forty-minute drive away. There was a light on in a window and an older man met them at the door. They were instructed to pull the van into the attached garage. Once the door on the garage closed, the old man had them carry Echo into the house. By then, she had lost so much blood that her skin was deathly pale.

After determining her blood type, the doctor asked Tanner and Henry what their blood types were. It turned out that Henry was a match; he donated a pint of blood. Echo left the house with Henry's blood in her veins, a leg with eight stitches, and an IV bag connected to her left arm.

She had remained unconscious, but the doctor felt confident that she would awaken before noon.

THE DOCTOR HAD BEEN CORRECT. ECHO'S EYES FLUTTERED open a little after nine a.m., in one of the bedrooms at the rented house. She stared at the ceiling for the first few moments she was awake, then she sat up in bed with such force that she nearly caused the IV stand to tip over.

"Whoa! Calm down. You're okay."

Echo looked to her right and saw Henry. He was rising from a chair in a corner of the room and was holding a laptop. Echo saw the gun holstered on his hip and her heart rate increased.

"Who are you?"

"I was going to ask you that question, and uh, you might want to pull up the blanket."

Echo looked down and saw that her breasts were exposed. Her head felt so woozy that she hadn't realized it. She covered herself with the blanket, then lifted it to look at her right leg, which was throbbing. The outer portion of the limb was purple and swollen where she'd been shot. And her shorts were gone as well. She was naked.

"You took my clothes off?"

"Your top was already off when I pulled you out of the water last night. The shorts and underwear were cut away when the doctor examined you."

"What doctor? Where am I?"

"A doctor treated you and you're on the mainland. What happened on the island last night?"

Echo remembered the scuba diver but shook her head. "You're not the man that saved me. That was Tanner. Where is he? Is he here?"

"You recognized him last night, right before you passed out. Why is that?"

"I met him before."

"He doesn't remember you."

"I was a child the last time I saw him, but I remembered him. He saved me then, and my mother."

Tanner had heard their voices. He entered the room and looked over at Echo. She sent him a bright smile.

"Hello, Tanner. I guess you don't remember me."

"Should I?"

"No. But maybe you'll remember my mom. Her name was Luna Grant."

"Luna?" Tanner said, and a memory sparked of a beautiful woman he had met many years ago, when he had recently become a Tanner. She'd been on the run from her murderous ex-husband, Steve Piper. Piper and his gang of thieves had been robbing an armored car company. The robbery failed and Piper and his gang had all died.

"I knew a woman named Luna who lived in California, I think the town was named Delran."

Echo's smile widened. "That was her. You saved her life, and mine too, I guess."

Tanner cocked his head and studied Echo. The makeup had been washed from her face and he could discern her features. "Luna had a young daughter. Was that you?"

"Yes. My name was Sofia then, now I call myself Echo."

"And your mother? What happened to her?"

The smile left Echo's face. "Mom died when I was fourteen. It was an undiagnosed heart condition."

"Did you kill Alex Bergman?"

Echo hung her head. "No. I had the bastard only feet away from me, but I couldn't shoot because he was using one of the prostitutes for a shield."

Tanner was pleased to hear that. Not only did it mean that Bergman was still alive, but Echo had spared an innocent woman's life while risking her own and letting her target survive. And it had been a target that was worth half a million dollars to her. The girl not only had guts, but she also had a heart.

"We took you to a doctor and he stitched up your leg and gave you a transfusion. He said you'll be weak, and you might limp for a time, but you'll be fine after a while."

"Whose blood did I get?"

Tanner gestured toward Henry. Henry had walked over to the bed holding clothes. They were a pair of his sweatpants and a matching blue sweatshirt, along with white socks. Echo looked up at him.

"What's your name?"

Henry was about to give her the phony name he was using, but then he shrugged. "I'm Henry."

Echo looked him over. "Since your blood is in me, I hope you don't have any diseases."

"I'm prone to get a headache if I eat ice cream too fast, but other than that I'm as healthy as a horse."

Echo nodded toward her left arm. "What's in the IV bottle?"

Tanner answered her. "It's something called Ringer's solution. The doctor said it would help with your blood loss. That bag is almost empty. You can unhook yourself from it, and there's a bathroom across the hall you can use."

Echo asked another question. "Why are you helping me? Having a doctor stitch me up couldn't have been cheap."

"I'm going to kill Alex Bergman. To do that, I need to know as much as possible about that island and the house he lives in. You've been there; you have knowledge I can use. Let me have that information and we'll be even."

"Of course, I'll help you. You saved my mother and now you've saved me." Echo laid her head back against the pillow. "I guess I did lose a lot of blood. I feel weak, and my leg aches like a bitch."

"Food will help that, along with the painkillers the doctor gave me to give you," Tanner said. "When you're ready, get dressed and join us. We'll be in the kitchen."

Tanner was walking out of the room when Echo called to him. "Tanner."

"Yeah?"

"I became an assassin because I want to be like you."

Henry laughed, said, "Welcome to the club," and he and Tanner left the room.

11
IF YOU FAIL TO PLAN...

TIM JACKSON HAD NEWS FOR TANNER. IT CONCERNED Bergman's attempt to beef up his security. Tanner had Tim's call on speakerphone so Henry could hear. Echo had eaten breakfast and then gone back to bed to rest. Her close call of the night before had left her in a weakened condition, while she had a pronounced limp from her leg injury.

"Donahue gets the guards they use from a company that specializes in offering their clients experienced private military contractors. When I was a kid, they were called mercenaries. This company, Defcon Security, refers to their people as 'Silent Professionals.'"

Henry smiled. "They'll be really silent if they get in Tanner's way."

"Who was that who spoke, Tanner?"

"That was Henry, Tim. He's the apprentice I told you about. He's helping me here."

"Hello, Henry. I hope we get to meet in person someday."

"Same here, Tim."

"Anyway, it looks like Bergman is upping his game. I think it's because they had another close call last night. From

what I gathered, a female assassin almost killed Bergman...
but Donahue sounded certain that she's dead, and that she
had a partner."

"She was working alone and she's still alive. Henry and I
saved her and now she's helping us by providing
information."

"You could use the help. Donahue is looking to hire
twelve more guards and has ordered some sophisticated
upgrades to the current guards' equipment."

"What sort of upgrades?"

"For one thing, they'll all be getting night vision equipment, along with something he called infrared beacons.
What are those?"

"The beacons can't be seen with the naked eye, but they'll
stand out to anyone wearing night vision. If the guards come
across someone who doesn't have a beacon, they'll know that
person doesn't belong."

"Oh, then I guess if you wear a beacon you'll be all right."

"Not necessarily. Some beacons can be configured to give
off different colored lights with the use of lenses, and the
rate of their flashes can be sped up or slowed down. That
way, the guards can change the type of signal the beacons
give off daily. If I showed up wearing an infrared beacon that
didn't match theirs, it would be like announcing to them that
I'm out to kill their boss."

"Hmm, this makes things a lot harder for you then,
doesn't it?"

"There's a way around that, but I'll need your help, Tim."

"Name it."

"I want you to break into the computers of the security
company Bergman is using. That way, we'll know exactly
how many guards they have and what they look like. Also, I
want you to add a new employee profile."

"Whose profile?"

Tanner looked at his apprentice. "Henry is going to join the enemy and become one of the new guards Bergman is hiring. With him on the inside, I'll have a better chance of defeating any security measures they take."

"Won't that be dangerous for Henry?"

"I can handle myself, Tim."

"If Tanner trained you, I don't doubt it, but still, be careful."

"How long will it take you to get inside their computers?"

"There's no way to know, but I'll get started right away. I don't expect it will take long. The company specializes in security but not cybersecurity. I'm guessing their firewall is no better than most companies. I'll get started now and let you know when I've got what you want. And oh yeah, I'll need you to send me a photo of Henry that was taken against a white background. I'll use that to build his phony profile."

"We'll send you one soon. And thanks. This would be much harder if we didn't have you helping us."

"Anytime, Tanner, you know that. I owe you for my life, and Madison's life. If you need me, I'll be there."

The call with Tim ended and Tanner and Henry began discussing their options. If Henry was to be placed on Bergman's security force, he could get close enough to the man to kill him.

Tanner shot down that idea. "Getting to him is only half the job. Getting away safely afterwards is more difficult. You can ask Echo about that."

"But they'll still think I'm one of the guards and would have no reason to suspect me."

"Donahue would suspect you and everyone else. Bergman isn't only his employer, but he's also his friend. Donahue will want revenge for Bergman's death. If he even gets a hint that you killed Bergman, you'd never make it off the island alive."

"How will you get off the island?"

"I don't know yet. I'll come up with a plan when I have more information."

~

Tanner received that information when Echo left her bedroom four hours later. She was still limping badly, but her skin had a bit more color to it, as she recovered from losing so much blood. She had been hungry again and devoured three slices of pepperoni pizza.

After leaving the kitchen, they settled in the living room. Tanner and Henry sat across from Echo in a pair of matching overstuffed armchairs, while Echo sat on the sofa with her wounded leg propped up on a cushion.

She smiled when Tanner asked her what she knew about the island.

"I know a lot. I've got detailed notes and photos of Bergman's house back at my motel room."

"How did you get photos of the house?" Tanner asked.

"They're copies of pictures that had been taken by the former owners. I tracked down the family that used to own Driftwood Island and broke into their home. They had an album of family photos that had been taken on the island."

"How did you break into the house? Are you skilled at bypassing locks and alarms?"

Echo laughed. "Sneaky is what I am. I snuck into the house while the weekly cleaning crew was there. They had the alarm codes and left the rear door unlocked after entering. I hid and waited until one of the crew cleaned the home office, then went in there and searched. Afterwards, I left before they reset the alarm. They never knew I was there."

"That's smart," Henry said.

Echo smiled at him. "Thank you, handsome."

"Tell us what you know for now, and then we'll go get the

photos and your notes. After that, you should leave before someone spots you."

"You want me to leave?"

"Yeah."

"I thought I could stay and help you."

"You're already helping. When I have those photos, you'll be helping even more."

Echo frowned. "I want to stay here until you take out Alex Bergman. That bastard and his men nearly killed me."

"Yes, they're trained killers who were defending themselves. And you were lucky to get as close to Bergman as you did. His friend, Donahue, was probably a good personal bodyguard, but he doesn't know much about security measures. That's why you were able to get to Bergman despite the lack of a plan."

Echo crossed her arms over her chest. "I had a plan. I pretended to be one of the hookers they had there."

"How did you know about the hookers?"

"I got lucky. When I was having lunch at a restaurant, I overheard two women talking about Driftwood Island, and that they were going there the next night. I followed them and discovered they were hookers, then I got the idea to go to the island and pretend to be one of them."

"If Donahue was better at his job there would be no way you could have been mistaken for one of the hookers they'd brought to the island. In fact, bringing those women there in the first place was a stupid idea. If Donahue was smart, that island would be locked down tight and he'd have boats out patrolling night and day."

"My plan still worked. I only failed because I didn't know Bergman wasn't alone in his bedroom."

"About this plan of yours, what preparations did you make for your escape?"

"I was going to leave the same way I reached the island, by swimming with the snorkel and fins I had."

"Why didn't you have them on when I found you?"

"There was no time to retrieve them. I was lucky to reach the beach without getting killed."

"And instead, you were shot in the leg. If Henry and I hadn't come along, you would be dead right now."

Echo let her arms fall to her sides as she looked down at the floor. "I know that. I-I guess I didn't plan well enough."

"No, you didn't. The man who tried to kill Bergman before you hadn't either; he's dead because of it. You need a plan when you go after a target like Bergman, then you need a backup plan. You also need to take other precautions, what my mentor called due diligence."

"I never had a mentor," Echo said. "But I've done six successful assassinations."

"Who were the six targets?"

"They were all open contracts on lowlifes. One of them had three men guarding him and I still killed him. I'm not a complete amateur, Tanner."

"I've been training Henry for years and he still has things to learn. If you want to survive as an assassin, you'll need to improve."

"You could teach me the way you're teaching Henry."

Tanner shook his head. "That won't happen, but... I might know someone who could help you."

"Who?"

"I'll let you know after I've talked to them and see if they'll agree. If they say yes, I'll introduce the two of you."

"Are they any good?"

"They've been an assassin longer than I have."

Echo smiled. "I'm willing to learn, and it would be nice not to be alone so much. I still talk to my old friends sometimes, but no way could I ever tell them what I'm doing.

They all think I'm a delivery driver." She struggled to her feet, limped over to Tanner, and kissed him on the cheek. "Thank you again for saving me. I'm lucky you didn't let me drown."

"I considered it, but then I realized you had information I could use."

"Oh."

Henry laughed at the look on Echo's face. "Tanner isn't running a charity. Why did you think he saved you?"

Echo shrugged. "Because I needed help."

"You were an assassin working a contract. You should never expect anyone to help you."

Tanner stood. "Henry's right. But now that you're here, we'll help each other. Henry will take you to get your things. While you're out, you might want to buy a cane somewhere."

Echo looked down at her leg. "I will. It hurts so much I can barely walk on it."

Henry and Echo left the house a few minutes later, after Tanner took a photo of Henry to pass along to Tim Jackson. Tanner watched them drive away, then he went for a walk along the rocky beach.

His mind turned to the island and the problem of getting away successfully after the hit was performed. With the addition of more guards and better equipment, it would be that much more difficult to escape.

Using a helicopter could work but ran the risk of being fired upon by multiple weapons. Stealing a boat was also an option; however, the risk would be great. The boat wouldn't be any faster than the other boats pursuing it, and certainly not faster than the bullets that would be sent their way.

There was also the added problem of the new guards Bergman was hiring. It brought the security force up past a total of thirty men. He had faced and conquered superior odds before, but Tanner was aware that he'd be pushing his luck to have that many people pursuing him across an expanse of water, where there was nowhere to take cover.

As he often did, he recalled strategies he had read of other Tanners using in the Book of Tanner. When he recalled a tactic that could be useful, he broke out in a smile. He refined the idea for his situation while coming up with other methods he could use if the main one failed.

When Tim called, Tanner wasn't surprised that the hacker had gotten past the security company's firewall in only a few hours. Tim was as good a hacker as Tanner was an assassin.

"I'll have Henry's profile added to their records by tonight, Tanner. I'll make it look good, but I can only give him so much experience since he's young."

"That's okay. Just make sure you place him in the batch of men being sent to guard Bergman."

"I was looking at that list. They're a hard bunch of soldiers for hire. Tell Henry to watch his back."

"Henry can take care of himself; he won't have a problem fitting in."

"So, he's going to be like you someday?"

"That's the plan."

"He has some big shoes to fill."

"So did I when I became a Tanner."

"Oh, I found out something else by listening in on Donahue's calls. He's sending two men to track down the woman who tried to kill Bergman. Actually, they're looking for her partner, since they believe she drowned."

"That means they're looking for Henry; he was the one that fired on them last night. They never knew I was there, and they never saw Henry's face either. By the way, I have that photo of Henry you wanted; I'll send it to you."

"Do that, and I'll get started on his fake employee file."

After talking to Tim, Tanner sent off a text to Henry.

Donahue has people out looking for you and Echo. Watch your back.

Henry replied with one word.

Always.

Tanner made another call. This time it was to New York City. A gruff voice answered.

"Hello?"

"Hello, Duke, it's Tanner. I need a few things."

"You name it, and I'll do my best to make it happen."

"For one thing, I need an invisible boat."

Duke chuckled. "I love it when you call. Next to you, my other customers are boring."

Tanner went on to explain what he meant, as his plan to kill Alex Bergman took shape.

FOLLOW NO MORE

HENRY AND ECHO DISCOVERED THAT THEY HAD SIMILAR TASTES in music as they drove to her motel room to pick up her things. On the way there, Henry stopped and bought Echo a wooden cane she could use to take some of the stress off her wounded leg.

She used the cane as she hobbled around her motel room gathering her belongings. Henry was surprised when he saw that Echo had three suitcases.

"That's a lot of stuff. How long did you plan to be here?"

"I've only been in Maine for a few days, but I travel all the time, since I don't have a real home."

"Why don't you have an apartment somewhere?"

"I don't need one, and I'm rarely in one place for more than a month. I love traveling and seeing new places."

"I'm the opposite. I like knowing where I'm going to lay my head at night."

Echo looked him over and smiled. "I'm sure you've woken up in a strange bed a time or two."

"Not as often as you might think. I haven't had a girlfriend in more than a year and work and school take up most of my time."

"You mean working with Tanner?"

"That's part of it, yeah."

"How did you get lucky enough to have him training you?"

"I met him when I was just a kid, then again years later when he saved me and some other people."

"He does that a lot, doesn't he?"

"Save people? Yeah, I guess he does. Ironic hmm?"

"He saved my mother from my psycho father who wanted to kill her. I was so young at the time, but I remembered Tanner, especially those eyes. Then, when I was a teenager, an older brother of one of my friends had a copy of this flyer that was going around. I couldn't believe it when I saw Tanner's face on it. That was when that cartel leader wanted Tanner dead. When I learned later on that Tanner had gone down to Mexico and killed that bastard, I thought it was so cool."

"He's incredible. And you're right, I'm lucky to have him training me."

When Echo finished packing, Henry took her bags out to the van. He and Echo were both unaware that there were men nearby asking about her.

∾

ECHO'S MOTEL WAS ON A HIGHWAY THAT HAD SEVERAL shopping centers and strip malls. The sporting goods store where she'd bought the snorkel and fins she'd used to reach Driftwood Island was on the other side of the highway from Echo's motel.

One of the guards had stumbled across the equipment and turned it over to Donahue. Donahue reasoned that the snorkel and fins had been bought recently and probably close to the island. He'd been right, and a young male clerk in the third sporting goods store that was checked remembered Echo.

"Yeah, I sold those to a cute blonde like three days ago. You know her?"

One of the men smiled at the clerk. It wasn't a nice smile, nor were his intentions. He was tall but his friend was short and packed with muscle.

"She came to a party on our island and left her stuff behind. We want to make sure she gets what she deserves."

"Deserves?"

"Yeah, you know, I'm guessing this stuff wasn't cheap. We'd like to give it back to her."

The clerk nodded. "That's cool."

"Did you see what she was driving? Or maybe we can get a look at your security tapes from that day."

"She didn't drive here. She walked."

"She must live around here then."

The clerk turned and pointed out the wide window that was behind the counter. "I watched her when she left. She crossed the highway and went over to that motel. The room she went into was one of the ones—oh look, there she is now."

The two men moved past the counter and stared out the window, where they saw Echo hobbling along slowly toward the van. Henry had just finished loading the last of her suitcases.

The tall man who had spoken to the clerk asked him another question. "Was she limping like that when she was here the other day?"

"No. I guess she had an accident."

"Or she was shot."

"What?"

"Nothing," the man said, as he and his muscular partner headed back to their car. There was a strip of grass dividing the highway, so the men had to drive to the nearest U-turn to reach the motel. If they had ridden over the grass, they might have attracted the attention of a cop and be held up while they got a ticket.

Henry was driving the van back onto the highway by the time they'd made the U-turn and neared the motel. The men followed.

"I bet that bearded bastard is the one that shot out our engines and killed Larry."

The short man nodded. "When we get a chance to kill them, I want the guy. Larry was a friend of mine."

"Hell yeah, we'll kill him, but Donahue wants us to bring the girl back alive if we can. I think he wants to give her to Mr. Bergman as a gift."

The short man balled his hands into fists. "I'm going to beat her boyfriend to death."

The tall man looked at his short friend and was glad he wasn't Henry. The man beside him was only five-foot-four, but he had enough muscle to tip the scales at two hundred pounds and he had seen him bench press more than twice that. Judging by the expression on his face, he was going to mangle the man who was with the girl before he killed him.

The tall man grabbed a satellite phone that was sitting in a cupholder and held it out for his friend to take. "Send Donahue a text and tell him we found the girl and the guy. I bet we get a fat bonus for this."

"Killing the guy will be my bonus."

~

HENRY BECAME AWARE HE WAS BEING FOLLOWED BECAUSE HE'D been watching for it. He made a stop at a gas station although the tank was three quarters full. He wanted to see what the vehicle he'd suspected was tailing them would do. When the car pulled across the street and parked in front of a house, he became certain and sent Tanner a text.

We've picked up two pests. How would you like me to handle it?
Tanner replied within seconds.
Where are you?
At the gas station we stopped at the other day.
Where are the men and what are they driving?
They're parked across the street in a silver Honda Prelude
Stay there. I'll join you.
Is something wrong? Echo asked.
"Don't look around, but we're being followed."
Echo tensed up, but she kept looking straight ahead. "Where are they?"
"Across the street. Tanner is on his way here."
"What is he going to do?"
"Kill them."

THE TALL MAN WAS A SMOKER. HE HAD LOWERED THE WINDOW on his side to let the smoke out as they waited for Henry to leave the gas station.

"They've been over there for a while."

The short man nodded. "He's inside the store buying drinks and snacks. Maybe they're taking a long ride when they leave here. How's our gas?"

"We're good; the tank is almost full. I just wish we had some food in case they drive for hours."

"They'll still have to stop for bathroom breaks. When they do, we'll get food."

The tall man sat up straighter. "Okay, he's coming out of the store. They should be heading back onto the road."

∿

HENRY HAD DELAYED LEAVING THE GAS STATION BY CHECKING his oil and visiting the station's attached convenience store. While in the store, he'd continued to watch the men who were following them, in case they left their vehicle and headed toward Echo. The men had stayed where they were and kept eyeing the van.

Henry knew it was about a five-minute drive to the gas station from the house. He figured Tanner would show up soon. As he got back in the van, he looked in the side-view mirror and saw that he was right. A hooded figure strode toward the men's car from the walkway of the home they were parked in front of.

∿

THE TALL MAN FLICKED HIS CIGARETTE AWAY AND WAS preparing to raise the window when a guy wearing a hood leaned on the door. The tall man noticed the silenced gun before he took in Tanner's intense eyes. Neither gave him a good feeling.

The short man had been looking the other way but realized that something had blocked the light coming in from the driver's side window. When he turned his head to look, he saw Tanner.

"Are you robbing us?" he asked.

Tanner held the gun in his right hand, but there was a phone in his left. It would send a prewritten text to Henry when he pushed a button.

"I know you're working for Alex Bergman. How did you track down the woman?"

The tall man looked disgusted. "Damn, you're with them. I was sure we weren't spotted."

"Answer the question."

The short man had turned red and was clenching his fists again. "We don't have to tell you shit."

Tanner sent off the text. It instructed Henry to blow his horn repeatedly.

The tall man jumped in his seat as the van's strident horn began blowing. He jumped again when Tanner fired the silenced gun and sent three rounds into the short man's torso, the slugs went through his thick muscle like it wasn't there. The color drained from the brute's face as his fists unclenched.

The tall man was leaning away from Tanner while trying not to touch the dead man slumped in the seat beside him. He was gasping for air, like someone who'd been running. Terror had that effect on people.

"How did you find the woman?" Tanner said again. He had to speak louder to be heard over the van's bleating horn.

The tall man told him about the snorkels and the fins while gesturing behind him. Tanner glanced at the floor of the back seat and saw the equipment lying in an open garbage bag. Along with the snorkel and fins was the green bathing suit Echo had worn during her swim to the island.

"Hand me the bag."

The tall man did so, as Henry continued to blow the horn and attracted the attention of everyone around.

Tanner took the bag and shot the tall man three times in the chest. The second round killed him by rupturing his heart.

As Tanner walked away, he sent Henry a text telling him that he would see him at the house.

97

HENRY FELT LIKE AN ASSHOLE AS HE BLEW THE VAN'S SHRILL horn and annoyed everyone around him, including himself, but he noticed that no one was looking in the direction of the car across the street. When the second text came in, he stopped blowing the horn like a fool and drove away.

Echo was looking back at the car. "They're not moving. They're dead?"

"They're dead."

"Wow."

"Yeah. Tanner doesn't mess around."

"Oh my God."

"What?"

"Last night, when I thought Tanner was one of Bergman's men, I tried to stab him when we were in the water together. I'm even luckier to be alive than I thought. He could have killed me."

"He could have, yeah."

"Alex Bergman is a dead man."

Henry made a left onto the street that would take them to the rented house. "Bergman was dead the second Tanner decided to kill him."

13
PREPARING FOR TROUBLE

DONAHUE RENTED SEVERAL MOBILE HOMES AND HAD THEM transported to one of the nearby islands Bergman owned. The surface of the island was small enough that you could walk across it in nine minutes. The shoreline had a strip of sand that was fifty feet wide. The rest of it was strewn with rocks. Bergman had bought the unnamed island and the others in the area the same time he purchased Driftwood Island. He was not a man who wanted neighbors about, although it was unlikely anyone would ever have attempted to build on the smaller isles, some of which were little more than sandbars.

Despite all the rocks, there was an area that was suitable for mooring boats, because someone had built a dock there years earlier. It was long enough to fit three or four boats, which suited their needs. To augment the boats, Donahue had rented a pair of jet skis. They could be used if the surf wasn't too rough and would make the short jaunt to Driftwood Island quickly.

Driftwood Island could be seen in the east. But all that

was visible of it were the tallest trees and the very top of the old lighthouse.

Originally, Donahue had planned to position more guards on Driftwood Island. He then realized that it wasn't necessary. It would be better to intercept a would-be assassin out among the small islands and keep them from getting near Bergman. The extra guards would also be close enough to respond swiftly if they were needed on Driftwood.

Those guards would number twelve, with four sleeping in each of the three trailers, although they would never all be asleep at the same time since they would be working different shifts.

The expense for the security was high, but it would be money well spent if it saved Bergman's life. And it would do that, Donahue believed. He now had over thirty men and they would all be equipped with night vision, bulletproof vests, and matching uniforms. The uniforms were green jumpsuits that had multiple pockets sewn into them. And thanks to the infrared ID markers each guard would be wearing, the men would know an intruder on sight even if they were clever enough to dress like one of the guards.

That was a tactic the man who first failed to kill Bergman had tried. He had been a big man carrying a rifle and wearing a tactical vest and he'd been walking around the property like he belonged. From a distance, and at night, he had looked like half the men guarding Bergman. If Donahue hadn't spotted the man as he neared the home, he might have fulfilled the contract on Bergman.

Thinking about that failed attempt on his friend's life made Donahue recall the second one. The girl had come closer to killing Bergman and now Donahue knew she had also survived. The two men he'd sent to find her and her partner had reported locating the pair, while stating that the girl was limping from a leg wound. Those men should have made contact again and weren't answering their phones. Donahue assumed they had been spotted and were dead.

He sighed. He didn't have as many guards as he thought, no, there were now two less, thanks to the girl and her partner. Whoever they were, they remained in the area. They would only do that if they were planning to make another attempt on Bergman's life.

Let them come. We'll be ready for them.

Donahue looked about at the small island as the men who had traveled there with him were busy stocking the trailers with supplies, including satellite phones for communication with Driftwood Island.

The new guards would be picked up on the mainland and brought to their post the next morning, where they would use the boats and the jet skis to patrol. That would make it that much more difficult for anyone to reach Bergman without being seen.

In the meantime, private investigators were hunting for James Horrigan. When he was located and dealt with, the contract would go away, and Bergman would be safe.

Donahue grimaced, recalling the girl and her male partner again. Bergman would never be safe until those two were found and killed. With the apparent failure of the men he'd sent to kill them, he would hire professional investigators to look for the pair, but he didn't expect they would be found.

He hoped they would be stupid enough to try to kill Bergman again. The girl was lucky the first time and he put a bullet in her leg. The next time he saw her, Donahue would place a round in her head.

TANNER TOLD HENRY THE PLAN HE HAD COME UP WITH WHILE Echo was unpacking her things in the guest room. When he got to the part about using an invisible boat, Henry laughed.

"How do you come up with these ideas?"

"The element of surprise is our greatest weapon as assassins. You always have to be thinking in unconventional ways that will shock your enemies."

Tanner went on to tell Henry the rest of the plan, including his part in it.

Henry was looking forward to going undercover.

"Since I'll be working as one of the guards, I'll be able to tell you what they'll be doing, and I'll sabotage them from the inside."

"Only we won't know anything until you're working with them. Which is okay. Duke won't be shipping the equipment here until tomorrow, and then I'll need a day to prepare."

"Does that mean you'll make your move in two days?"

"Yeah, but not until that night. According to the weather forecast, there will be a chance of fog. That weather will make things easier for me and tougher for the guards."

Henry looked in the direction of the guest room. "What about Echo? Do you trust her?"

"I believe she's told us the truth, but no, I don't trust her completely."

"I want to trust her, but we don't know enough about her."

"That's why we won't let Echo know what the plan is. She failed to kill Bergman and collect the half a million-dollar contract. But she would know that Bergman would be willing to pay for information about a coming attack."

Henry frowned. "I hope she's whom she seems to be; I'd hate to have to kill her."

"So would I," Tanner said.

The door opened on the guest room and Echo came

hobbling out while using her cane. She had changed out of the clothes Henry had given her and was wearing a bright yellow skirt with a white top and red sneakers.

"I feel better wearing my own clothes."

"You look better too," Henry said, as he eyed her. The tight blouse accentuated her breasts while the skirt revealed her shapely legs, although the wounded leg was still swollen and bruised.

Echo spoke to Tanner. "I know I can't do much because of my wound, but let me know if you need me when you decide to go after Bergman."

"You can help by showing me those photos you have of the island."

Echo had brought along her purse, which had been in her motel room. She reached into it and took out a phone.

"Those photos are all here, but this is a small screen."

Henry pointed at the large flatscreen TV. "We can transfer them to the television."

Echo looked at him. "You know how to do that?"

"Yeah, it's easy, since the TV is a later model, and we have Wi-Fi. Just bring up the photos and I'll show you what to do."

"You can show me too," Tanner said, as he was always willing to learn.

Henry showed them how to cast the photos onto the TV's screen. There were dozens of photos that had been taken several years earlier before Bergman had owned the private island.

The former owners had been a family of six. They were smiling in every photo they were in and gave the impression they were a tight-knit bunch. Tanner was looking past them and taking in the details of the property.

The house and the surrounding grounds had been built on a manufactured hill to avoid flooding from the sea. The mound had been created with a gentle slope that extended to the edge of the land that had been cleared when the home had been planned.

Echo had also copied several videos showing an aerial view of the island. Those had been taken from a drone the youngest member of the family had received as a birthday gift one year. The drone footage was invaluable in helping Tanner to refine his plan, particularly regarding the due diligence he would employ as a precaution against being caught or killed by Bergman's guards.

After looking at all of it twice, Tanner told Echo to send everything to his phone, so he could view it all again whenever he wanted.

"I hope that helps you come up with a plan," Echo said.

"It will," Tanner said, without going into detail about how it might be used.

Echo yawned and used her cane to stand. "I'm going to take a nap. I'm still feeling weak from the blood loss, and the painkillers make me drowsy."

"You may be alone when you wake up. Henry and I have errands to run."

"I'll be fine. If you order food for later, I'll pay for it. And I vote for anything Chinese. I love Chinese food."

Echo disappeared into the guest room and shut her door.

Henry looked at Tanner. "Is it smart to leave her alone here?"

"I've set up cameras, so I'll know who comes and goes from the house. If she makes a call or sends a text, Tim Jackson will know about it after I give him her phone number. He'll also be able to track the phone if she goes on the move with it."

"Having a hacker working for you is a handy thing."

"My plan wouldn't work without him, including the part where you pretend to be a guard."

"It will give us a chance to know what Bergman's security is like inside and out."

"Watch your back when you're there. You'll be with men who are willing to do whatever is asked of them, if it pays well enough."

"I'll be careful."

Tanner stood. "Let's get going. I've several stops to make. One of them will be to a toy store."

"Why?"

Tanner smiled. "I can't go home empty-handed; Lucas and Marian will be expecting gifts when I return, and so will Sara. It's a tradition."

"You miss them, don't you?"

"Yeah, but we'll be heading back home in a few days."

"And Alex Bergman will be dead."

"Oh Yeah."

14
KID'S GOT GAME

Henry arrived early at the meeting place where the new guards were to assemble. It was a restaurant that had gone out of business and had a For Sale sign on the door. With the tables, chairs, and booths gone, what had been the dining room area was now a large open space. Alex Bergman had bought the property after it was foreclosed on. He had plans to renovate it and sell it for a profit. The restaurant had served seafood for over a decade; a slight scent of cooked fish lingered in the air.

There were three other new guards already there when Henry arrived. Greeting them at the door was Donahue and four of the guards from Driftwood Island. Donahue looked taller than he had in the two photos Henry had seen of him, and his blond hair was worn short.

The established guards and the new men worked for the same company, Defcon Security, and most of them already knew each other. The other new guards showed up on time and Donahue addressed the gathering as they stood in a semicircle before him.

"I know you were told that you would be staying on

Driftwood Island, but there's been a change and you'll be posted on one of the smaller islands that's not far from where your employer lives."

One of the men spoke up. He was forty, tall, muscular, and had a shaved head with a bushy red beard. An arrogant scowl seemed to be his perpetual expression. Henry had heard him referred to as Mason.

"I'm not going to sleep in some damn tent."

"It won't be a tent," Donahue said. "There are trailers on the island. They have propane and are hooked up to generators."

"And how dangerous will it be?" Mason asked.

"There are people who want your employer dead. They won't mind killing you to get to him. If that scares you, then leave now."

Mason huffed. "Nothing scares me. But I'd feel better about things if you weren't hiring guys who had no experience."

"I was assured you all had experience and were ready to face anything."

To Henry's surprise, Mason pointed at him. "There's no way that guy is experienced. Beard or no beard, he looks damn young."

"Worry about yourself," Henry told him.

Mason cocked his head and grinned. "Are you talking back to me, boy?"

"I don't give a shit about you. I'm here to do a job and get paid."

Mason looked around the room at the other men. He had worked with many of them before, and some were his friends.

"This kid is looking for an ass whupping."

A few of the men laughed, and several gave knowing nods. They were aware that Mason was a bully who liked to intimidate those he deemed weaker than himself. It wasn't surprising that he would choose young Henry to be his newest victim.

One of the other men, Sanchez, called over to Henry. "I know you think you're tough, kid, but you don't want to mess with Mason."

Henry *didn't* want to mess with Mason. He wanted to fade into the background and not stand out. That was no longer an option thanks to the loudmouth with the red beard. Henry could back down from a confrontation and be thought a punk, or he could stand up for himself and risk having to fight the man. If he had to fight, he was certain he'd win. He had been instructed in hand-to-hand combat by Tanner initially, and later learned more from Casey Rocco, the man who ran the Parker Training Center. Casey Rocco was one of the deadliest men in the world when it came to unarmed combat. Henry had mastered many of the skills Casey taught.

Despite that, Henry tried to deescalate things by speaking to Donahue. "Are we here to protect the client or to fight each other?"

Donahue was no help. "Maybe Mason is right, and you're too young. If you're worried about your fellow guards, you might run for cover when the shooting starts."

Henry pointed at Mason. "I'm not worried about him. If we fought, I'd put him on his back in five seconds."

Several of the men who knew Mason laughed, and so did Mason. He sauntered over to Henry, said, "You ain't nothing but a punk," and raised a hand to shove him.

Henry slapped the hand away and rammed his shoulder into Mason's chest with enough force to send the man stumbling backwards. Henry followed up with a flurry of punches to Mason's stomach, then pressed a forearm against his throat while hooking a foot behind his left knee. Mason lost his balance and landed on his back. It hadn't taken five seconds; it had only taken three. The men who had been laughing now wore expressions of shock.

Mason sprang to his feet. His face was turning as red as his beard, and his teeth were bared.

Henry issued a warning. "Back off or I'll hurt you."

Mason put his fists up and moved in to throw a punch. Henry raised his hands as if he were going to do the same, then pivoted and sent a kick into Mason's face. The big man grunted as blood flowed from a busted lip. A second kick missed, as Mason leaned away from it, but a third kick landed against his stomach and made him bend over, which left his face exposed again. A hard right broke Mason's nose and sent him to the floor. Henry followed him down and delivered an elbow strike to his throat. He held back on the force he employed. He wanted to disable the man, not kill him.

Mason's face was a bloody mess and he wheezed loudly with each breath he took. Henry stood and appeared no different than he had before the fight started. His breathing was normal and there wasn't a mark on him. He looked around the room.

"Is that enough experience for you?"

Sanchez, who had warned Henry not to fight Mason, was now shaking his head in wonder. "The kid's got game."

When Mason made it to his hands and knees, Henry offered to help him stand. Mason slapped his hand away and stood on his own. Henry shrugged, and Donahue told the four men he'd brought with him to start handing out the uniforms.

15

INVISIBLE BOAT

TANNER RECEIVED A CALL FROM HENRY AND TOOK IT IN private while walking on the beach. Echo was back at the house watching TV. After they'd left her alone the day before, she'd made no calls and had no visitors, which meant she'd given Tanner no reason not to trust her.

Henry was calling from inside the car he'd driven to the restaurant. Donahue had told everyone to grab their gear and Henry used the opportunity to give Tanner an update. He had begun the call by saying two words. "I'm in."

"How close will you be to Bergman?"

"There's been a change. I'll be living out on one of the small islands instead of being on Driftwood."

"What's the location?"

"I don't know yet, just that we'll be on one of the other islands. My guess is that it will be the closest one."

"You'll be on your own until you can contact me again. Watch your back."

"I'll be fine. I can handle myself."

"You can, but you're also inexperienced at working undercover. If you make one slip or give them a reason not to trust you, things could go bad for you in a hurry. I'm having second thoughts about letting you do this."

"Tanner, Cody, I can do this. I just don't know when I'll be able to make contact again to let you know what's going on."

Tanner was quiet and Henry waited, knowing he needed time to make a decision.

"Okay. Stick with it and call me when you can. But if I don't hear from you within two days, I'll come looking for you."

"I'll find a way to contact you, and I'll have information that can help. So far all I've learned is that the guards will now be wearing green coveralls and we'll be patrolling around the island on boats and jet skis."

"Be careful, Henry. No contract is worth your life."

"I'll stay safe, but I have to go now; the other men are heading for the vans that will be taking us to the dock."

"I'll be waiting for your next call."

"You'll get it. Goodbye."

Tanner ended the call and looked up to find Echo waving to him from the rear deck of the house. He raised a hand to acknowledge her and began walking back. Echo had slept a lot the previous day and said she felt better. She was still hindered by her wounded leg, but that would heal in time.

She smiled at Tanner when he joined her on the deck. "Were you talking to Henry?"

"Yeah."

"Will he be back soon?"

"No. He had something to do and won't be back for a few days."

"Oh. I was going to ask him if he wanted to go for a ride somewhere; I'm getting bored just sitting around."

"I'm going out; you can come with me."

"Where are we going?"

"I have a package to pick up," Tanner said. Duke had come through and the items and equipment Tanner had ordered were waiting for him at the warehouse of a shipping company. He didn't have it sent to the house to avoid anyone having the address. He trusted Duke, but it was good practice to take precautions and maintain security.

TANNER THOUGHT OF SOMETHING WHEN THEY WERE IN THE van and headed to pick up the delivery.

"Do you have a vehicle, Echo?"

"Yeah, a rental. It's not far from here."

"We could pick it up on the way back."

"I'd like that. I just hope I can work the pedals without screaming. My wound hurts like a bitch whenever I flex my leg."

"Flex it anyway, or you might lose mobility."

"Have you ever had a leg wound?"

"Yeah."

"Was it as bad as mine?"

"It was, but I had also been shot in the back and the chest."

"Holy crap! You must have come close to dying."

"I did. When I got back on my feet, It took time for my leg to heal right, since I hadn't been walking on it. I know it hurts, but exercise it as much as you can, or you'll pay for it later."

They were quiet for a while, then Echo spoke. "My mom never forgot you. I showed her one of those flyers that was being passed around when Alonso Alvarado was out to get you. Mom said you would be all right, that you would outsmart Alvarado."

"He was outsmarted, but the plan I used had been thought up by a friend of mine."

"Tanner."

"Yeah?"

"Were you and my mom ever... close?"

"If you're asking if we had sex, the answer is no. I only knew her for a few hours, remember?"

"I don't remember much at all, except for your face, and those eyes of yours; I was only about three or four then."

"You look like her."

"I do, but she was prettier, and man how I miss her. She died too young."

"Some of the best people do," Tanner said, while thinking about his family, who Alvarado had slain when Tanner had still been a teenager.

DUKE HAD SENT EVERYTHING IN A WOODEN CRATE. THE NAME of the recipient was stenciled on the crate as Aaron Butcher, or A. Butcher. Duke had a sense of humor.

They stopped to get Echo's car on the way back after making certain no one was staking it out. She was able to drive it despite the pain that came with moving her foot to press down on the pedals.

They separated when she told Tanner she would go shopping for food. She was particular about coffee and the brand they had at the house wasn't to her liking. Tanner let her go. She wasn't a prisoner, and he didn't have a reason to distrust her. If she met up with someone, or made a call to someone, he would learn about it from Tim Jackson. And besides, he wanted to be alone when he opened the crate inside the home's garage.

The crate contained a sculpture that was itself a container. If the authorities had opened the crate for whatever reason, they would have found a sculpture that was a fair representation of Mount Rushmore, although much smaller.

Tanner took the same crowbar he had used to open the crate and smashed in Abraham Lincoln's head. The sculpture was hollow and contained the items Tanner had ordered. After removing everything he'd expected to find, he discovered that Duke had thrown in a bonus, as he often did. They were a pair of flat knives that were made to be strapped to the inside of your forearms. Tanner appreciated the gesture.

Once he was sure he had everything he ordered, he changed into swim trunks and left the garage. He was going down to the water to test his invisible boat. It wasn't actually a boat. It was a waterproof device that had a strong motor and a powerful sound system. It could be guided by remote control or be made to run on one of several settings. The top of it was covered in a reflective material that would mirror the water it would be placed in.

Tanner waded into the surf and lowered the device into the water after turning it on. When it dipped below the surface he wondered if he had wasted his money, but then he realized that the top of it was still visible. You had to be right up on it to make it out.

As it was made to do, the motor kicked in fifteen seconds after being activated. A recessed propeller dropped down and the device headed away from the shore. The sound of the small motor was joined by a recording of bigger ones as the speakers came on. Tanner lost sight of it as it moved away, but he heard what sounded like a boat with twin outboard motors and the slap of waves against a hull. The noise was loud and would carry a great distance. Tanner closed his eyes and listened. If he hadn't known better, he would have thought there was a boat nearby.

After opening his eyes, he looked around and saw an older couple standing on the patio of a house that was two doors down from the one he was staying in. They were looking out at the water. The woman held her hand above her eyes to cut the glare, while the man was gazing through a pair of binoculars. They were searching for the boat they could hear but couldn't see.

After a short, animated conversation the woman threw her hands up in frustration while the man scratched at his head. They were confused and bewildered. The guards at the island would also be confused and they would chase Tanner's "invisible" boat. Since he was going after Bergman at night, the darkness would help the effect even more.

The boat's sounds faded as the device went farther out to sea. After ten minutes passed, Tanner wondered if it had sunk. It hadn't. A few minutes later, he could hear it as it drew closer. The sound it made was only the noise of its own engine. As programmed, the speakers had cut off as it made the return trip. The motor powering it shut off when sensors revealed it was in shallow water, and the waves brought it to shore sixty feet from where it had been launched. It was powered by a battery that would need to be recharged.

A former CIA toymaker Duke knew had created the gadget at Tanner's request. It had cost sixteen thousand dollars. Four thousand of that was compensation for it being a rush job. It was worth every penny and would aid him in making a successful escape after he killed Alex Bergman. Instead of chasing after him, the guards would be busy hunting down a phantom boat while he headed off in a different direction.

~

ECHO RETURNED ABOUT AN HOUR LATER WITH FOOD AND supplies. She was surprised to find Tanner in the kitchen preparing dinner.

"You can cook?"

"I can, but I don't do it very often. This is just a simple casserole that we can throw in the oven later. I'll make hamburgers for lunch."

"Cool. And I just bought some buns and potato salad we can have with them."

Echo had left the kitchen to use the bathroom when Tanner's phone rang. He frowned when he saw the call was from Tim Jackson. He wondered if Tim had bad news to deliver concerning Echo's activities while she'd been away from the house. Tim wasn't calling about Echo; he had other news.

"A private detective agency Bergman hired has located James Horrigan, Tanner."

"Did they say how?"

"Horrigan's daughter used her cell phone to text a friend, and she mentioned to her that she and her father were in Naples, Florida. Donahue is sending two men there to find Horrigan."

"What's the daughter's phone number?"

"I'll give it to you, but I tried calling it and only get voice-mail. I left a message saying I was a friend of her father's and that I needed to speak with him."

"I told Horrigan no phone calls, but I guess his daughter broke that rule."

"If those men find him, they'll kill him, and maybe his daughter too."

"I know, Tim. See if you can find out how the men are traveling. My guess is that they'll be flying commercial."

"They are. I already checked. Their plane leaves in thirty minutes. It's a direct flight."

"It won't take them long to find Horrigan. I have to assume the private detective agency will still be looking for Horrigan, to pinpoint his exact location. Once they have it, they'll pass that information to the men out to kill Horrigan."

"How can I help?"

"I have to get down to Florida again. I'll use the same jet service I did last time. Find out how soon they can get me to the Naples area."

"I'll look into it and call you back."

"Thanks, Tim."

Echo had returned as the conversation was ending. She saw by Tanner's expression that something was up. "What's wrong? Is Henry okay?"

"It's not Henry who's in trouble. It's the man who brokered the contract on Bergman. Donahue sent two men off to kill him. If he's dead, the contract goes away."

"Whoa! Where's the guy at?"

"He's in Florida. I'll be headed there soon."

"I'll go with you."

Tanner was going to say no, then decided he would take Echo along.

"Go pack a bag. We'll be leaving soon."

Tanner wasn't taking Echo along because he wanted the company. He was taking her along to test her. If she failed, she'd never leave Florida alive.

16
THE TEST

MASON GAVE HENRY DIRTY LOOKS DURING THE BOAT RIDE OUT to Driftwood Island. Henry ignored the red-bearded fool and concentrated on listening to a conversation Donahue was having with Bergman on the satellite phone.

Donahue was assuring his boss that the new security guards would soon be settled in and that he had good news to tell him when they spoke in person.

Henry wondered what that good news was and hoped it didn't concern Tanner. Donahue had left two of the four men he had with him back on the mainland after receiving a call that made him smile. Henry was concerned that they might have tracked down Echo again. If so, he knew Tanner would handle any trouble that came along.

They were going to Driftwood Island before settling in at their base on one of the smaller islands, so that all the old guards could get to know the faces of the new men, and vice versa.

Henry would use the opportunity to take in as much detail as he could. The photos and videos that Echo had were great, but also years old. Bergman must have made changes in the time he owned the island.

They landed at the dock and Henry had to keep from smiling when he saw that two of the boats there had new motors attached. He had been the one who destroyed the old ones on the night Echo made her attempt on Bergman's life.

There were four boats where before there had been only two. Like the increased number of guards, more boats were a security enhancement.

Henry liked Echo, but the woman had only made Tanner's job more difficult by her failed attempt. Bergman was spooked, having come so close to dying; the new safeguards he had in place would make it twice as hard for Tanner to get to him. What had started out as a tough contract was turning into a challenging one because of bad luck.

Yes, the hit was difficult, but not impossible. By being on the inside, Henry could assist Tanner and warn him of any traps that might be laid out for an assassin.

There were four guards waiting for them by the dock when they arrived. They were already wearing the new green uniforms. It gave them a professional appearance.

Henry and the rest of the new guards were escorted to the house along a winding trail that was one he didn't remember seeing on the drone video taken of the property. He realized why when it was explained that the path was new. Donahue had ordered it be laid out and they were told that it was the only safe way to reach the house from the shore, other than to cut through the surrounding woods.

There were two other trails nearby that ran through the trees. Sanchez mentioned them and asked why they couldn't be used.

"They've been turned into traps," Donahue told him. "The men dug a pit along each of the other trails. If someone walks on them who doesn't know better, they'll break through the thin boards we placed over them and covered with sand."

Sanchez frowned. "You might trap a lot of animals too."

Donahue shook his head. "It's unlikely, the boards will support about sixty pounds before they break. There aren't any animals on the island that weigh that much."

"How deep are the pits?" Mason asked, his voice sounded nasal because of his busted nose, and the skin around his eyes was turning black due to damaged blood vessels.

"The pits are eight feet deep and have wooden spikes at the bottom. If someone falls in there, we're sure to hear their screams."

After being shown around the island, the new guards were lined up along a corridor inside the house. Bergman came down the stairs to greet them. It was important that he recognize the guards and that they knew him on sight as well.

Henry was close enough to reach out and grab the man as Bergman walked past him. When Bergman reached Mason and saw his damaged face, he asked what had happened.

"Two of the men had a disagreement," Donahue told him. "It's been settled."

"Who did he fight?"

Donahue pointed toward Henry. "The young one there."

Bergman walked back over to Henry. "Are you a troublemaker?"

"No sir. I was defending myself."

"You're supposed to be defending me. If there's any more trouble you'll be replaced, understood?"

"Understood," Henry said. As he was speaking, he was imagining placing a bullet between Bergman's eyes.

∽

AFTER BEING TAKEN BY BOAT AROUND THE ISLAND TO LEARN the routes they would patrol, the new guards were settled on a smaller nearby island. Henry never did learn what the good news was that Donahue had to share with Bergman. He only hoped it wouldn't affect Tanner.

~

THE GOOD NEWS WAS THAT HORRIGAN HAD BEEN LOCATED IN the Naples, Florida, area. Once he was dead, the contract on Bergman would go away. Tanner and Echo were traveling to Florida to keep that from happening.

Echo had never flown on a private jet and was impressed. When she asked Tanner for more details about where they were going, he fed her false information, while keeping things close to the truth.

He told her that the man who brokered the contract on Bergman was staying at an address in Naples, Florida, and that it was important that he get there before someone killed the man.

"I've learned that Bergman is using a different middleman to offer a reward of a hundred thousand dollars to anyone who locates the broker. He has people in the area, but so far they don't know where he is."

"A hundred thousand dollars? That's a lot of money just for information."

"It's not that much to a man like Bergman. He'd gladly pay it to have the contract cancelled."

Tanner's story about Bergman offering a reward was a lie, but Echo didn't know that. If she were eager to get her hands on the money by revealing Horrigan's location, Tanner would give her every chance to do so.

The truth was that he had no idea where Horrigan was, only that he was likely living on his boat. That was the one advantage he had over the men looking for Horrigan. They, and the private detective agency Bergman hired, would spend time searching for Horrigan in hotels. That delay might be enough to allow Tanner time to track down Horrigan first.

Of course, that was only a guess. If the private detective agency was aware of Horrigan's boat, they might locate the man and his daughter at a marina. If that happened, the trip to Florida would be a waste of time and Horrigan could be dead when Tanner found him. If so, it wouldn't save Bergman, as Tanner would still kill him, and have a personal reason to do so.

He and Horrigan were never friends, but he had worked with the man at one time and had respected Horrigan before his addictions took hold of him and ruined him. There was also Horrigan's daughter to consider. If she were found with her father, as she surely would be, she would be murdered alongside him. If that happened, killing Bergman would be a pleasure.

As their flight continued, Tanner asked Echo to tell him about the contracts she had fulfilled. She described them in detail. Most of the targets were lowlifes such as pimps and drug dealers who'd had small contracts taken out on them.

Echo had been successful at killing them because they never considered her to be a threat. As a good-looking young woman, it never occurred to them that she could be an assassin. That was fine, but it would only work against amateurs. A professional bodyguard suspected anyone who came near their client, or they should. Echo's luck had held again when she went after Bergman. If the guard outside his bedroom had been a true pro, she would have never made it within twenty feet of Bergman, would have been discovered to be pretending to be a hooker, and would have died.

Echo had survived through a combination of luck and

pluck. She would need to gain several skills if she were to be successful long-term.

Although, if she didn't pass the test Tanner was laying out for her, she wouldn't survive the day.

That test involved a file folder Tanner carried with him. He told Echo that it contained the address where Horrigan was staying and that there was information concerning the contract on Bergman, along with contact info for the broker handling the reward.

"My hacker worked up a complete profile on Bergman. I even have the man's phone number and shoe size. Once I've made sure the go-between is safe and the contract is still on, we'll return to Maine and deal with Bergman."

During the flight, Tanner left Echo alone with the file while he went into the bathroom. If she were thinking of claiming the reward on knowing Horrigan's whereabouts she'd have every opportunity to do so by reading the phony file. If she attempted to reach out to the broker handling the reward for Horrigan's whereabouts, she would be contacting Tim Jackson instead. Tanner would know then that Echo couldn't be trusted.

TANNER SEPARATED FROM ECHO AT THE AIRFIELD BY PLACING her in a taxi and telling her to get them rooms at a hotel in Naples. He would call her later after he made the drive to the house where Horrigan was staying, but first, he had to take the time to sign out the vehicle he had rented over the internet.

Tanner was pleased when Echo asked to come with him, but she would realize he would decline the offer, because of her injured leg.

"No. You get a hotel room and wait for me to call you. I

may have to move fast, and you can't do that because of your wounded leg."

Echo looked disappointed, but it could have been an act.

"Call me as soon as you can, Tanner. I'll be worried about you."

"I will," Tanner said, then he had helped her into a cab and watched her ride away.

BACK IN MAINE, HENRY WAS ASSIGNED TO BUNK WITH Sanchez and two other men. The four would never be in the trailer at the same time since they were paired off and would be working twelve-hour shifts. Those shifts wouldn't begin until the next day, so some of the guards would be sleeping elsewhere for one night. Those men would be on fold-out cots in the mess hall. Two of the men were given night vision binoculars and had been assigned to keep watch for boats in the area.

Henry would be working with Sanchez and had been given the night shift, which he would start the next day. Henry was glad when he learned that Mason would be on the day shift; it meant that he wouldn't have to interact with the man.

He had made an enemy in Mason and wanted as little to do with him as possible. As for Sanchez, he was the quiet type who seemed to keep to himself. The two of them worked well together doing their part to help assemble a large metal storage shed that would be used as the mess hall. They had been assigned the task by Donahue along with two other men. The rest of the guards did other tasks, such as erecting the temporary showers, and setting up a grill.

When they were done, the building looked good, although it rattled in the wind coming off the ocean. Still, it would keep heat in and rain out while they ate their meals. The food would be delivered three times a day from Driftwood Island, where they had the basic kitchen facilities Echo had reported seeing.

They had their first meal outdoors while they were still putting the shed together, and Henry had seen Mason pointing his way while talking to two other men. Henry wondered if the red-bearded thug was planning something, if so, he'd handle it.

Donahue announced that the first day shift would begin the following morning at eight a.m. but that anyone assigned that shift would be expected to be at their post fifteen minutes early. The same would be true for those on the night shift, who were scheduled to begin their shifts at eight p.m.

Henry preferred to work the night shift since Tanner would be fulfilling the contract on Bergman at night. Day or night, it didn't matter. He would be able to help Tanner whenever he came. What did matter was finding a way to contact Tanner. Normal cell phones didn't work on the island; Henry needed to gain access to a satellite phone.

Donahue kept one in the small trailer he was using as an office. Donahue's trailer was empty, while Donahue was off the island. Henry had plans to break in there and use the phone. What he didn't know was that Mason had plans of his own, and those plans ended with Henry being found dead.

17
FAILURE

Thanks to Tim Jackson, Tanner knew that the men Donahue had sent after Horrigan had landed in Florida less than an hour before he had. He'd assumed they would waste time checking out hotels but that proved to be wrong.

The private detective agency that was helping to track down Horrigan had uncovered the fact that Horrigan owned a boat, and that the vessel was no longer docked back in Sarasota. Instead of checking out hotels, the men were searching marinas while looking for Horrigan's boat, the *Beth Anne*.

There were over two dozen marinas where Horrigan could be tied up or he could be out for the day on the boat. Luckily, Horrigan had told Tanner he'd be using an alias, unfortunately, the *Beth Anne* didn't have an alias. Once the boat was spotted by the men, it would only be a matter of time until they had Horrigan.

Tanner was told at the fifth marina he visited that he was the second one to ask about the *Beth Anne* that day. He was wearing dark sunglasses to hide his memorable eyes.

"The man who asked, how long ago was that?"

The guy gave a little shrug. "Maybe half an hour ago."

"What did he look like?"

"Um, about your height, a little younger than you, and oh yeah, he had on a Boston Red Sox T-shirt. I teased him about that because I'm a Yankees fan."

Tanner smiled. "That sounds like my friend. Was he with another guy?"

"Yeah, a dude with lots of hair."

"That's them. I've been trying to track them down, along with our friend who owns the *Beth Anne*. What were they driving?"

"I don't know; I only talked with them for a few minutes."

Tanner thanked the man for his help. When he stepped out of the dockmaster's office he headed to his car and drove back to the last place he had visited. He had been traveling south while visiting marinas. He wondered if the man in the Red Sox T-shirt and his hairy friend had been traveling north.

He returned to the marina he had been at before and saw a guy with long hair and a heavy beard pull out of the parking lot and head right. Seated next to the man was a guy wearing a red T-shirt. Tanner was too far away to make out whether the shirt had a logo on it, but he thought he might have located the two men Donahue had sent to kill Horrigan.

They must have asked about the same boat he had only a short time later. They were probably informed that someone else had been asking about the boat as well.

He took a chance and followed them. When they pulled into the parking lot of another marina twenty minutes later, he was certain they were the men. It was confirmed when they left their vehicle and he saw that the red T-shirt had a Boston Red Sox logo on it. The other man was hairy. Along with the long hair and beard was thick hair covering his forearms.

They went to the office and inquired about the *Beth Anne*. When they came out, they were looking around in an apprehensive manner. They were aware that someone else was after their prey but didn't know why. It worried them.

The hairy man took out a phone and made a call. Tanner imagined he was phoning Donahue and asking him if he had sent someone else to find Horrigan. When the answer came back as no, they might assume it was the private detective doing so.

Tanner had brought along a tracking device. He attached it to the men's vehicle and then followed them on foot as they walked about the marina.

Tanner knew Horrigan hadn't been at the marina when he was there earlier asking about the *Beth Anne*; that didn't mean he might not have arrived there during his absence.

He hadn't. The men walked past all the boat slips and Horrigan's vessel wasn't docked in any of them. When they returned to their car, the men left the parking lot and headed north again. Tanner followed.

IT WAS GETTING DARK BY THE TIME THE TWO FINISHED searching the last marina. For all they knew, Horrigan could have recently docked at one of the marinas they had checked out earlier. Attempting to find Horrigan by physically searching marinas was a tough way to go about it and prone to failure. What they needed was more information, and the same was true for Tanner.

Horrigan's teenaged daughter had gone against her father's instructions and used her phone once; it was likely she would do so again. Tim Jackson was able to track her through her phone, apparently, Donahue's private investigators could do the same.

If the girl used the phone again, it would be a race to see who would get to Horrigan first, Donahue's men, or Tanner.

Of course, Tanner had the advantage of being able to track the men. Where they went, he went. Once they made their move to kill Horrigan, Tanner would be there to stop it cold.

The two "silent professionals" drove to a restaurant that was near the last marina to get a bite to eat. Tanner did the same, while sitting alone at the bar. As he ate, he kept an eye on the men by watching them in the long mirror that was behind the bar.

He had rushed to Florida believing that Horrigan was in imminent danger, now it looked like saving Horrigan's life could take time. He hoped not. According to the weather forecast in Maine, there was fog rolling in tomorrow night around Driftwood Island. That would be a great time to make a move on Bergman, as the haze would obscure movement and block out the moon's natural light.

While thinking of Maine, Tanner wondered how Henry was doing.

HENRY WAS RESTING IN HIS TRAILER WITH SANCHEZ. THEY HAD both put in a day of work erecting the metal shed and had gone on to practice using the jet skis. While that was fun, it had also been tiring. They were ready for sleep and would have to rise early to attend training on Driftwood Island.

Henry wasn't sure how he felt about Sanchez. The man handled his share of the work, but he kept to himself and didn't seem interested in being friendly. Henry didn't blame him. As armed guards protecting a client who had a price on his head, they were there to make money, not friends.

The trailer had been modified to hold a set of bunk beds.

Although the beds would be used by the men on the day shift as well, they would be able to change the sheets and blankets before bedding down for the night.

Henry had claimed the top bunk. After locking the door on the trailer and turning off the lights, Henry climbed up into his bunk to go to sleep. It took a while; his mind was active going over everything he had learned and observed on Driftwood Island. He was eventually lulled to sleep by the persistent hum of the nearby generators.

AN HOUR LATER, THE TRAILER DOOR OPENED AFTER ITS CHEAP lock had been picked. Henry had stirred awake when he heard the door's squeaky hinges. Below him on the lower bunk, Sanchez reached out and turned on a light. The trailer shook as three men entered. They were all armed and carrying their guns at their sides. At the forefront was Mason. He grinned at Henry.

"It's time for payback, boy."

Sanchez climbed out of his bunk and held his hands out. "I don't have anything to do with this."

"Yeah, you do," Mason said. "You're going to back up our story that this asshole snuck out and came after me, then we chased him back here, and when he pulled a gun on me, I shot him."

Henry hopped down from his bunk; he only had on boxer shorts. He gestured at himself.

"Who's going to believe I went outside like this? And look, I'm barefoot."

Mason glanced down at Henry's feet, just as one of those feet rushed towards him. Henry landed a kick against Mason's chest and sent him stumbling into one of the men behind him. After making the kick, Henry whirled and sent a second kick into the face of the remaining man; it sent the guy backwards and he landed on top of Mason. Henry claimed the third man's dropped gun and aimed it at the men as all three sat up.

"Try anything and I'll shoot you," Henry told them.

The scuffle and the light being on had attracted the attention of the two men who had been assigned to patrol; they appeared in the doorway of the trailer and one of them asked what was going on.

Henry spoke as he lowered the weapon he was holding. "Mason wanted a rematch, but this time he brought help along."

"That's a damn lie!" Mason shouted. "We caught this kid sneaking around and chased him back here. I think he was coming after me, or maybe he's working for someone who's out to get Mr. Bergman."

The man in the doorway released a sigh as he brought out a satellite phone. "I'll let Donahue figure this mess out."

~

DONAHUE ARRIVED TWENTY MINUTES LATER BY BOAT. HE DID not look happy to have been roused from his bed on the other island. By the time he arrived, Henry and Sanchez had dressed and were outside the trailer with Mason and the others.

Mason repeated his lie about having found Henry skulking about and said that he looked like he was up to something.

Henry denied it and gestured toward Sanchez. "Ask him what happened. He and I were both asleep when Mason and these other two broke into the trailer."

Donahue looked at Sanchez. "Who's telling the truth?"

Sanchez glanced at Mason, then pointed at Henry. "I saw

him sneak outside, and then he came running back here with Mason chasing him."

Henry gawked at Sanchez. "What? Why the hell are you lying?"

Sanchez looked away, unable to meet Henry's eyes.

"I've heard enough," Donahue said. He glared at Henry. "Gather your things. You're out of here. We don't need a troublemaker around."

Henry opened his mouth to protest then decided not to because it would be a waste of time. He left the trailer with the duffel bag he'd brought to the island. As he walked past him, Sanchez whispered.

"Sorry, kid. I need this job and Mason has a lot of friends."

Henry sent him a "Fuck you!" look and let himself be escorted to one of the boats. Forty minutes later he was back on the mainland where he'd left his car and was watching the boat head back.

He had failed. He was supposed to be working undercover as one of Bergman's guards to help Tanner and he hadn't even lasted a day.

Henry drove toward the rented beach house feeling like a failure and knowing he had let his mentor down.

18

BACK SEAT SHOOTER

Tanner had followed Donahue's men after they'd left the restaurant. They checked into a motel near Route 41 only to leave it a few minutes later. Tanner had to assume they had received the same information he had.

Horrigan's daughter had used her phone again. Tim Jackson said she had sent a text to a friend and mentioned the marina they were headed for. It was one of the ones Tanner had visited earlier in the day and was some distance away from where he currently was. He followed Donahue's men there and waited for the boat to arrive. According to the girl's text message, they would be getting in just before midnight. That meant they were about an hour away.

Saving Horrigan was taking longer than Tanner had thought it would; the good news was that Echo hadn't revealed herself to be untrustworthy.

If she had read the file Tanner had left out in the open on the plane, she hadn't done anything with the information. Tanner called her to give her an update. She asked if he needed her to do anything.

"There's nothing to do until I locate the broker."

"I thought you knew where he was?"

"I was mistaken. I have found the two men who are here looking to kill him. At least, I think that's who they are. They might also be men who are working for a private investigator."

"How are you going to know the difference?"

"I'll talk with them. I've grown tired of following the men around."

"Be careful."

"I will be."

After ending the call with Echo, Tanner sent off an email.

This is Tanner. Where are you?

There was no response. That wasn't surprising, given the late hour. He was about to put away his phone when he saw that he had received a reply.

I'm in Caracas. I'll be flying back to the United States in the morning. Do you need help?

I want to talk to you about something. Where will you be?

My flight will be landing in Miami at noon for a layover. From there I'm headed to Chicago for more work.

I'll meet you in Miami. Text me when you arrive.

Does this concern work?

No. I need a favor, a big one, if you're willing.

I owe you. The favor is yours.

Don't decide until you know what it is. See you tomorrow.

With that done, Tanner eased out of his rental wearing a cap pulled down low and headed toward the car being driven by Donahue's men. At least, he assumed they were Donahue's men.

There were people around regardless of the late hour. An older couple was seated on the deck of their boat talking quietly, while a party was breaking up on a barge where the hosts were saying goodnight to their guests. It was a young group and many of the women were good-looking.

The hairy one was behind the wheel of the car he'd been driving earlier, while his partner was seated next to him and had a pair of binoculars. He was checking out one of the partygoers who was wearing a short black dress.

Neither man noticed Tanner until he knocked on their window. The hairy man was startled by the sound and flinched. He was glaring at Tanner with annoyance as he lowered the window.

"What do you want?"

"Relax, we work for the same people. Michael Donahue called the office and said he wanted to make sure nothing went wrong, so they sent me to help you."

"You work for Defcon Security?"

"Yeah, Mr. Murphy had me down here handling a special project. Now he wants me to help you guys out here."

The man in the Red Sox shirt leaned over to get a better look at Tanner. "If Murphy sent you, then that means you know our names."

"I don't know who's who, but one of you is Rick Taylor and the other is named John Mazzulla."

"I'm Mazzulla," the hairy man said, and he and the other guy relaxed visibly. Murphy was the name of the man who managed operations at Defcon Security. By mentioning his name, and their own names, the men assumed Tanner was legit. What he was, was lucky to have Tim Jackson working for him. Tim had gathered the information he needed. By knowing Murphy's name, they had answered a question for Tanner. He now knew for certain that they were Donahue's men and not private investigators. The investigators were hired to locate Horrigan, not kill him. Tanner would have spared them had they been investigators. But these men were out to kill Horrigan. He couldn't allow that to happen.

"Let me climb in the back; I don't want to attract attention."

The car's locks clicked, and Tanner opened a door and slid onto the rear seat.

Red Sox turned around to speak to him. "This guy Horrigan should be here soon. John and I were planning to wait until two a.m. and then go on the boat. By then, the marina should be nice and quiet."

"If you shoot the target that will make some noise."

"We'll handle the target. His daughter is on the boat. Once we hold a gun to her head, he'll do anything we want. John can drive the boat. He'll take us out to sea and that's where we'll torture Horrigan to have him give up the money."

"That makes sense. It also sounds like I won't have much to do."

The hairy man, Mazzulla, looked at Tanner by using the rearview mirror.

"The client is giving us a fat bonus for this, but we're not splitting it three ways."

"Relax. I'm just here as a supervisor because the client is getting nervous."

Red Sox laughed. "You'd be nervous too if someone had taken a contract out on you."

The party guests had all left. On another boat, the people who had been sitting out on their deck went inside.

The *Beth Anne* came into the marina at 11:47. Horrigan docked the boat expertly and tied her up. Red Sox looked at Horrigan through the binoculars then passed them over to his hairy partner. Horrigan's daughter, Beth, was above decks; the hairy man commented on her.

"That girl looks older than seventeen, and she's good-looking."

Red Sox gave his friend a sideways glance. "Don't get any ideas, John."

"Hell no. I'm not a damn teenybopper rapist, I'm just

saying. And we'll make it quick and painless when her time comes. You know, because she's a kid."

"We won't have to torture Horrigan to get the money. I bet he gives it up hoping we won't hurt his daughter."

The two were into sports. They discussed various teams and players while they waited for two o'clock to arrive. Tanner commented occasionally, although he rarely watched sports and didn't follow any teams.

When he was offered chewing gum, Tanner accepted a stick; he didn't want the gum, but had a use for the soft foil wrapper it came in.

When there was no one in sight, the Red Sox fan left the car and took care of the two cameras that were on poles and aimed at the slips. The cameras were too high to reach, but the wiring powering them was at ground level. When he was done, the guy returned to the car. Their plan was to wait until two a.m. to board Horrigan's boat, and they were sticking to it.

By 1:17 the marina was as quiet as a cemetery, other than the soft lapping sounds made by the water and the squeak of the ropes as they stretched and grew slack from the boats they secured, which were cradled in their slips.

Feeling that the time was right, Tanner tore his gum wrapper in half and wadded up the pieces, then he slipped them into his ears. With that done, he eased out his sound suppressed weapon and went to work doing what he did best. Red Sox died first. Tanner had shot him in the back three times before swiveling the gun toward the hairy man. The hairy man, Mazzulla, was looking down at the gun when it went off. Tanner fired three more times and the slugs hit Mazzulla in the side. The man moaned and reached for the weapon that was concealed under his shirt; the hand slid away before he could grab the gun. His neck went limp, and his bearded chin settled on his chest.

Blood was beginning to pool on the vehicle's floor but none of it had splattered the windows since Tanner had directed his shots downward. The wads of foil in his ears were removed, having served their purpose. Although the shots were suppressed, the sound of them was still loud inside the closed confines of the car.

Tanner sat back and waited to see if anyone had heard the suppressed shots and would come up on deck to investigate. Someone did; it was Horrigan.

That was not surprising. The man had to be on edge and might have still been awake. Tanner saw him look around while keeping one hand hidden behind his back. It was a safe bet he was holding a gun in that hand.

Tanner stayed where he was. If he stepped out of the car to get Horrigan's attention the nervous man might take a shot at him before he could identify himself. And if he called out it would wake others.

Seeing nothing amiss, Horrigan went back below. Tanner left the car, retrieved the tracking device from beneath it, and walked over to the boat to board it.

Horrigan would have felt the boat shift and come up to investigate. He did so, and as he stuck his head up, Tanner called to him in a quiet voice.

"It's Tanner, Jim."

Horrigan had been startled by the sound of his voice and gasped. Realizing who had spoken, he came up on deck while tucking his gun in his waistband. His voice was a whisper as he spoke.

"Shit, you scared me. What are you doing here?"

"Is your daughter asleep?"

"Yeah. She went scuba diving today. That always makes her tired and puts her out like a light."

"She was awake enough earlier to send a text to a friend of hers. That message was tracked by Alex Bergman's private investigators. His man Donahue sent two operators here to kill you."

Horrigan stared at him for a moment. "Those men aren't a problem anymore, are they?"

"No."

Horrigan ran a hand through his hair. "I'm sorry. Beth must have used her phone while I was showering earlier."

"If I hadn't flown back down here to help you again, you and your daughter would have had a very bad night."

"Oh God."

"Yeah. Now listen, there are two men dead in a car in the parking lot. I'm going to leave them there to be found. When the police question you, play dumb. My guess is that they'll eventually assume it was a drug deal that went bad."

Horrigan spread his hands. "I don't know how I'll ever repay you but name your price and I'll come up with the money."

"I don't want your money, Jim, and this will all go away soon. By this time tomorrow, Alex Bergman will be dead. In the meantime, wait around here until the cops say you can leave. And remember, use your real name."

"Okay. And Tanner, thanks again, man."

Tanner sent Horrigan a nod and walked back to his car. After leaving the marina, he pulled over during the ride to the hotel and reattached the license plate onto the car.

At the hotel, he stopped by the desk to get a key card for the room Echo had secured for him earlier.

He was looking forward to calling home in the morning and talking to Sara and the kids. He missed his family and was tired of thinking about Alex Bergman. What should have been an easy hit and a learning experience for Henry had developed into a tougher contract with various complications, such as Horrigan, Echo, and Lou Lazio.

Tanner showered and got into bed. He was asleep by two-thirty and would be up at eight, when he would make a phone call home to the ranch.

He'd meant what he'd told Horrigan. When he left Florida, he would be headed back to Maine to kill Alex Bergman, then escape the island and head for home.

What Tanner didn't know, was that fate had other plans for him.

19
GOODBYE AND GOOD LUCK

Tanner was smiling when he ended his call to Sara. The smile stayed in place when his phone rang, and he saw that the call was from Henry. But when Henry spoke, Tanner could hear the sadness in his voice.

"What's wrong? Are you in danger?"

Henry sighed. "I screwed up. I was sent packing and I'm no longer one of the guards."

"But you're safe?"

"Yeah, I'm good, but useless. I was supposed to be your inside man and I didn't even last a day."

"Tell me what happened."

Henry explained his initial confrontation with Mason, and Sanchez's later betrayal. Tanner listened as he spoke, but only asked a question once. When Henry was done, Tanner commented.

"I wouldn't have done anything differently."

"Seriously?"

"Yeah."

"I thought you'd be disappointed."

"It's not ideal that you're no longer a guard, but things

have been going wrong with this contract from the beginning. You were there for a while though, tell me what you've learned."

Henry did so and found himself talking longer than he would have thought. He described the differences he had observed between the way the island appeared in the photos Echo had given them, and the way it was now.

"That will all be a big help. I can tell you were observant."

"I tried to be. When are you coming back here?"

"I'm flying out at two. Echo won't be with me."

There was silence on the line, then Henry said. "She failed the test you set up for her?"

"She passed. How do you know about the test?"

"Tim Jackson called me after learning that the guy I was pretending to be was sent packing. He wanted to make sure I was all right and we started talking. I like Tim; I hope to meet him in person someday."

"He's the best there is at hacking. His skills are going to make this contract easier to complete than it would be if he weren't helping us."

"So, if Echo passed the test why won't she be back here?"

"I'm hoping she accepts an offer I'll be making."

TANNER AND ECHO WERE AT MIAMI INTERNATIONAL AIRPORT to meet someone. When the woman appeared, Echo wore a shocked expression.

"She's old."

"You might want to call her mature."

"And she has your eyes. Are you related to her?"

"We're cousins," Tanner said, and then he smiled in greeting as Elke Gant walked over to them.

Elke smiled back at him then shifted her gaze to Echo. "I see you didn't come alone."

"This is Echo. She's the reason I have a favor to ask you."

Elke smiled at Echo. "Hello, young lady; my name is Elke Gant."

"Is that a German accent?"

"It is."

"I've always wanted to go to Germany, and France, and the UK too."

Tanner gestured toward a coffee shop. "Let's sit down and talk."

TANNER EXPLAINED HIS IDEA OVER COFFEE. ECHO WAS inexperienced and needed training, while Elke had decades of experience and no one to teach it to. Why not travel together and work as a team for a while?

Tanner knew from experience that the life of an assassin could be a solitary one, and both Elke and Echo had expressed to him separately that they were lonely at times. In Elke's case, she was still mourning the loss of her only son, and Echo lacked a mother figure in her life.

The two women looked at each other, then Elke spoke.

"I could use a traveling companion, and I do have much knowledge about our profession that I could pass on."

Echo looked down at the table. "I know I'm inexperienced and have been lucky so far. If it wasn't for Tanner, I'd be dead. If you're willing to teach me, Elke, I'm willing to learn."

Elke smiled at her. "We'll take it one day at a time and see how it works out."

Echo looked up with a smile on her face. "I'd like that."

Tanner took a ticket from his pocket and held it out to Echo. "Elke is headed to Chicago. I'd like you to go with her."

"Today?"

"My flight leaves in about an hour," Elke said.

"I guess I could go. But what about my car back in Maine?"

"It was rented under a fake name. Just leave it behind. You're already packed, and your things are out in the car."

Echo shrugged. "Yeah. Okay, I guess I'm headed to Chicago."

"If this arrangement doesn't work out for either of you, that's fine. I just thought you might want to give it a try."

"We will do that," Elke said.

She and Tanner continued to talk while Echo went out to the car to grab her belongings. Tanner reminded Echo to leave her weapons behind.

Elke asked about Sara and the children, then she assured Tanner that she would keep his true identity a secret from Echo.

Tanner filled her in about Echo's past. It didn't take long since the woman was so young.

"I will call you soon and let you know how we are getting along. I hope it works out; it will be nice to have a companion. And I can teach the girl what she needs to know."

"I enjoy having an apprentice, maybe you will too."

"How is Henry doing?"

"He exceeds my expectations on a regular basis. It won't be long until I've run out of things to teach him. After that, he'll go out on his own."

Their departure time arrived, and Tanner told them goodbye. Echo surprised him by giving him a hug.

"Tell Henry I said goodbye and that I'll see him again someday."

"I'm sure he'd like that, and so would I."

The plane to Chicago took off on time. Tanner left the terminal and walked to where the private jets were. He was in the air a short time later and headed back to Maine. A check of the weather forecast revealed that fog was still expected in the region containing Driftwood Island, and there was also the possibility of a thunderstorm before morning.

The fog would help, as it would make it more difficult for the guards to see him. All systems were go. As far as Tanner was concerned, Alex Bergman had only hours left to live.

20
RUN FOR YOUR DEATH

Henry was disappointed to learn that Echo had left, but he was glad to hear that she had gone off with Elke Gant.

Tanner was back in Maine and eager to get to work. With Henry at his side, he gave the invisible boat another test run and decided on what setting he would need to lure the boats off in the wrong direction.

With a storm approaching, the ocean was more turbulent than it had been but still navigable. Tanner needed to infiltrate the island, kill Bergman, then make his exit swiftly, before the storm made traveling on the water too dangerous.

Henry would be at the helm of the boat while Tanner handled the equipment they would use. Their first destination was the island where the new guards were stationed. To get there, Henry took them out to sea past the chain of small islands containing Driftwood Island. They would then circle back, cut the engine, and let the current take them in. If done right, they would wind up on the opposite end of the island where the new guards had their trailers. No one traveled there. The guards made regular trips around Driftwood Island as part of their duties, but not their own small island.

They had the mindset that they were the fierce protectors of their client, Alex Bergman. It never occurred to them that they themselves might need protection.

With Henry's expulsion, there were eleven new guards remaining. If the schedule hadn't been changed, five or six of them would be out patrolling, while the rest of them would be in the shed that had been constructed to act as a mess hall. They would be having a meal before their evening shift started. The lying bastard Sanchez would be one of those men.

After securing their boat by using a simple fluke anchor, Tanner and Henry lowered themselves into water to walk onto the shore. They were dressed in full body wet suits that left only their hands, feet, and faces exposed. Black boots covered their feet, ultra-thin black gloves their hands, and night vision goggles hid their eyes.

They reached the other side of the small island in minutes. There were gas generators in operation and the sound of them was loud, while their exhaust placed the scent of gasoline in the air. The trailers were nearby and connected to the generators by extension cords.

Tanner and Henry made a methodical search of the trailers in case someone was in them. They determined they were all empty and moved toward the mess hall. They could hear voices coming from the shed. Judging by the aroma drifting out, the men were having a dinner of grilled fish.

They had lowered the goggles since there was plenty of light inside the small compound. When Henry opened the door of the shed, he saw Sanchez seated with the others. He had just enough time to register the look of recognition in Sanchez's eyes before Tanner tossed in a flash-bang grenade and the door was slammed shut.

The tin shed rattled tremendously from the blast as the

men inside cried out in alarm. The metal walls of the shed helped to heighten the sound of the detonation and the sudden brilliant light must have left the men seeing spots before their eyes.

The door was opened again, and Tanner and Henry fired on the men with suppressed weapons. Henry made certain that Sanchez died by his hand.

Afterward, Henry led Tanner back to the trailer that was used by Donahue when he was on the island. It contained supplies, including the green jumpsuits the guards wore.

TWENTY-TWO MINUTES LATER THEY WERE STANDING ON THE dock wearing the jumpsuits as they awaited the return of the guards who had been out on patrol. To keep their faces hidden from view, they were bent over and pretending to look at an engine on the remaining boat, as if it wasn't working and needed to be repaired.

If all were well, that boat would have left the dock already to begin patrolling while the day shift returned.

Tanner killed the first man who drew near by shooting him as he eased his boat up alongside the dock. Henry tied off the bowline to a cleat before rejoining Tanner to wait for the next boat to arrive.

Tanner looked over the equipment the man had been using and determined that the IR flasher was red and blinking on and off at a rate of one flash every second. Instead of adjusting his own to do the same, he took the one the man had and gave it to Henry. Its former owner no longer had a use for such things, or any other thing.

Tanner would get an IR flasher for himself from one of the other returning men. There would be no reason for them to have their night vision goggles on since the dock area was well-lit.

Later, if they were spotted by anyone wearing night vision as they approached Driftwood Island, the guards there would see that they had the correct IR signal and would believe they were two of the new men out on patrol.

Instead of one boat appearing next, the last two came back together. When Henry saw that Mason was in the boat at the rear, he told Tanner that the red bearded man was his.

As the boats pulled up, Tanner killed his two men while Henry handled the other two. Mason's companion died quickly with a shot to the head, but not Mason. Henry had taken careful aim and placed a round in Mason's gun arm.

The big man bellowed from the pain and his eyes went wild with fright. Mason leapt from the boat and onto the dock, where he stumbled and fell onto his knees. His wounded right arm was bloody and hanging limp, and he had to raise himself up using only his left. Henry caught him on shore as Mason was trying to grab the holstered gun on his right hip with his left hand. The gun slid free of the holster but was fumbled and fell into the water.

Mason tried to fend off Henry's attack; he was no more successful than he had been during their first confrontation. Henry pummeled the man with punches until he went down, then he dragged him deeper into the water and held him beneath it as the waves battered them both. Mason drowned at Henry's hands. The body was left to drift onto shore like so much garbage.

When Henry rejoined Tanner, his face was set in stone. "Let's go kill that bastard, Bergman. I'm sick of being here."

Tanner nodded once, turned, and walked back to where they'd left their boat.

If Bergman had been relying on his new guards to keep him alive, he was out of luck.

DONAHUE WAS IN HIS ROOM INSIDE THE HOUSE ON DRIFTWOOD
Island and was looking out at the thickening fog. He had a
bad feeling that he couldn't shake.

He'd been informed that the two men he'd sent down to
Florida, Rick Taylor and John Mazzulla, were dead. That
meant that Horrigan was still alive and that the contract on
Bergman was active.

What bothered him was that he didn't know who had
killed the men, but he couldn't imagine it had been Horrigan.
The man was a go-between for assassins, not an assassin
himself. He had assumed that Horrigan had gotten lucky and
killed the first man he'd sent after him, but it would have
taken more than luck to kill two experienced operators like
Taylor and Mazzulla.

Along with that, the girl he'd wounded the other day was
still out there somewhere with her partner. It seemed a
certainty to Donahue that they would make another attempt
on Bergman's life, or else, why had they stayed in the area?

The one bright spot was the new guards and the regular
patrols they had started running. It would be tough for
anyone to make it to the island without being spotted by one
of the boats. The sound of their boat's motor alone would
alert the men.

As he had the thought, the sound of an actual motor
could be heard off in the distance. Donahue checked his
watch and realized that the new guards had begun their
night shift. He wondered how long they would be able to do
that. A weather alert had come in saying that the thunderstorm that had been expected to stay out at sea until morning
was moving inland sooner than anticipated. If the water
became too rough, the patrols would have to be placed on
hold until the storm passed.

Donahue grabbed his satellite phone to call the guards stationed on the other island. If they had to dock their boats and forego the patrols, he wanted them to do so on Driftwood Island, to increase the number of guards present.

No one answered the call. A worried frown appeared on Donahue, but he wasn't concerned yet. Given the heavy cloud cover rolling in, it was possible that the satellite phones might fail to work. Possible, but not likely. A sense of dread began after he tried calling the other phones he had handed out to the new guards and received no answer. His anxiety lessened a little when a call he made to a guard on site was answered.

"Yes, sir?"

"I haven't been able to contact the new men. It could be the weather making it difficult to reach them by phone... or it could mean we have trouble headed our way."

"I'll alert the men who are off-duty and tell them to get into their uniforms."

"Yeah, do that, and send two men here to the house to increase the number of guards watching the home's perimeter. I'll be in Mr. Bergman's room."

"Yes, sir."

TANNER AND HENRY MADE IT TO THE ISLAND AND WERE dressed like the other guards, including the IR flashers that identified them as being one of the troops. They stood out anyway. Henry was burdened with the fake boat, which he wore strapped to his back; the thing weighed about eighty pounds.

Henry kept his back as straight as possible so he wouldn't walk stooped over, if he had his head down, it would be harder to keep watch for any guards they might run across.

Carrying the heavy machine while walking in wet sand was making each step more difficult, but they needed to stay at the edge of the surf to leave no trace of their footsteps behind. The going was made slower by the fog, but the mist also obscured their movements.

Tanner carried less weight than Henry but was toting along the items he needed to fulfill the due diligence he had planned for this contract. If something went wrong, the precautions he was taking would increase his chances of survival and escape. The invisible boat was in that category as well but was also part of the plan.

They left the surf after reaching the eastern shore of the island, where the old lighthouse was located. The fog was dispersing as rain moved in. Henry left the invisible boat in the sand just past the reach of the waves, and he and Tanner slipped into the cover of the trees to wait for one of the patrolling guards to come along.

One appeared eight minutes later and came to a stop as he spotted the strange object lying in the sand. After looking around warily, the man headed toward the invisible boat with his weapon in his hand. He was a few yards away from it when a voice called to him.

"Hey Jerry, what's that?"

The first guard, Jerry, had jumped after being startled. He recovered his composure and answered the question as the second guard began walking toward him.

"I don't know what it is. It could just be some junk that washed up on shore."

The second guard aimed a flashlight beam at the package and spotted the footprints around it. "Someone left this here. I think we have an intruder. I'll call it in."

As they watched from the trees, Tanner whispered to Henry. "You kill the first man and I'll kill the second."

Henry answered by raising his silenced gun and taking

aim. The guard named Jerry went down from a shot to the head as the other guard did the same. Tanner had killed the man as he was bringing up his radio to call in an alert. The two bodies were left where they fell. It was just a matter of time until someone noticed they were missing; having them be found was a part of Tanner's plan.

Tanner patted Henry on the shoulder. "You know what to do. Be careful and I'll meet you back at the boat in less than an hour. If I'm not back by then, it means I've had to make a change to the plan. If that happens, you leave, and we'll meet up tomorrow at the house."

"I could stay and help you."

Tanner shook his head. "No. You'd be outnumbered and possibly fighting alone, because I might have to hunker down somewhere until I can find a way off the island. Stick to the plan, Henry."

"I hear you."

They separated, and Henry prepared to launch the invisible boat, while Tanner was off to increase his chances of surviving. If he were wounded and couldn't make it back to the boat, he would have to hide. He decided that the nearby area where the driftwood was located was a good spot, as it offered more than a few places to get out of sight. There were several damaged skiffs and other small, shipwrecked boats there that he could crawl beneath. In preparation for that contingency, he placed food and water there, along with a spare gun, and a small explosive device he could arm and use if it became necessary. He then left similar provisions at another place.

Only once did he see a patrolling guard, and the man was walking with his head down against the rain that had increased in its intensity.

The concealing fog had dispersed as the wind began gusting. In the east could be seen flashes of lightning, as the sound of thunder grew louder with the storm's approach to the island. Tanner had been counting on the fog to aid him, but its absence wouldn't derail his plan.

When he was done with his preparations and ready to make his move, he stood among trees and took in the house. The area around it was well lighted and there were lamps on inside.

Two men were on guard on the covered porch, with one seated on each side of it. Because there was plenty of light, they had their night vision goggles off. They were staying quiet and would take turns making a trip around the house four times an hour. The guards hadn't been there when Echo had made her attempt on Bergman's life. At that time, there had only been a single guard left outside the door to Bergman's bedroom. That had been a wooden door with a regular lock. The new door was made of steel. It required a correct four-digit code be entered into a keypad to release the electronic locks built into it.

It still wasn't much security and little challenge for a man like Tanner. No, what made the contract difficult was the aftermath of the hit. Getting off the island and away safely presented unique problems. Tanner's use of the invisible boat should aid greatly with that, and having Henry along made things that much easier.

Tanner assumed that Bergman was inside the house, but for the plan to work, he needed to know where Donahue was. He checked his watch and saw that there was less than two minutes to go until Henry caused a disturbance. He would do so by firing off his gun along the eastern shore of the island, right after he'd activated the invisible boat. That would lure Donahue to that location and away from Bergman.

Afterward, Henry would return to the spot on the southern shore where they'd left their own boat and wait for Tanner to join him. And while Donahue and the others were off chasing a phantom boat, he and Henry would escape in a different direction.

The key was to make sure that Donahue and Bergman weren't together. With Donahue being the hands-on type, Tanner felt certain he would rush off to investigate the gunshots along with the guards.

As if thinking of the man could make him appear, Donahue emerged through the front door of the house and spoke to the two guards. Tanner was glad to see him away from Bergman. It was the first bit of luck he'd had on this contract.

The time arrived and Henry shot off his gun several times without using a sound suppressor. The noise didn't carry as well as it might have because the wind was increasing. The gun was loud enough though, and it made Donahue reach for the radio on his hip as he took off toward the eastern end of the island. Before leaving, he shouted to the two men on the home's porch to stay sharp. A few seconds later, an alarm began to blare, signaling that there was trouble.

Tanner gave Donahue time to reach the eastern shore and begin his pursuit of the phony boat. He needed the man far enough away so he wouldn't hear what was about to transpire at the house. When he thought sufficient time had passed, Tanner stepped out of the trees with his weapon up. He shot the man standing on the right side of the porch then did the same to the man on the left.

They had each been hit in the chest twice. Although their bulletproof vests had spared them from being wounded, they had done nothing to alleviate the pain caused by the force of the slugs slamming into them. Both men released groans and collapsed to the floor of the porch.

Tanner could have shot them in their heads while both were standing. Had he done so, one of the slugs might have passed through and shattered a window behind them. If that had happened, it would have alerted the man who was standing guard outside Alex Bergman's bedroom.

Before the men on the porch could recover, Tanner was standing over them, and this time he did shoot them in their heads.

That left the entry to the house unprotected, but Tanner didn't enter. He had no intention of going inside. He was going to bring Bergman to him, thanks to the hacking skills of Tim Jackson. Tim had hacked into Donahue's satellite phone and had also spoofed the number.

Tanner took out a satellite phone and dialed the number of the one Bergman owned. During his walks on the beach over the last few days, he had practiced imitating Donahue's voice, which had been captured on recordings. Thanks to Tim, the satellite phone he was using would display the same identifying information as the phone Donahue was using. If Tanner could successfully imitate Donahue's voice, Bergman would have no reason to doubt he was talking to his old friend.

Bergman answered on the second ring. "Is something wrong, Mike?"

Tanner spoke in Donahue's voice, and there was a sense of urgency in his words. "Alex, get out of the house. There's been a bomb planted in it. Get out now! Now!"

"Wh-what? A bomb?"

"Yes, damn it. Stop talking and run. You've got only seconds to get out of there."

Tanner heard Bergman say something unintelligible that might have been a curse. Beeping sounds were made as Bergman disengaged the electronic locks on his bedroom door, then there was the click of the door being opened. That was followed by Bergman telling the guard outside his room about the bomb.

If the guard was confused or skeptical it didn't stop him from following a panicked Bergman, who was racing down the wooden stairs. The thumping of their footsteps could be heard over the phone and then the noise was near enough to hear out on the porch, because Tanner had disabled the alarm and picked the lock to be able to crack open the door and listen.

The men came into sight with Bergman in the lead. He was a match for photos Tanner had seen of him, only his hairline had receded, and his face was a little fuller. Being stuck inside the house had probably put a few pounds on him. Soon, concerns about his weight would no longer be a problem.

Bergman leapt the final three steps, stumbled, but regained his balance and sprinted toward the door. Tanner swung the door open and raised his gun.

The guard died first because he was armed and carrying a rifle. Tanner sent three rounds at the running man and two of them struck home. One of the bullets entered the man's left cheek and the second one tore apart his throat.

Bergman never slowed and rushed past Tanner while shouting. "There's a bomb!"

The man was so terrified he failed to register the fact that his guard had just been shot to death behind him.

Tanner took aim at Bergman's back and sent three bullets after the panicked fool. Bergman went down as if he'd been struck by a sledgehammer. When he walked over to him, Tanner saw that Bergman was still alive. He had on a bullet-proof vest beneath his shirt.

Alex Bergman turned over and stared up at Tanner. His terrified expression had turned into a grimace of pain, only to morph to panic as he realized his death was imminent. He held up a hand.

"I'll give you anything!"

Tanner fired twice at Bergman's forehead and the contract was fulfilled.

21
CRACK! BOOM!

HENRY HAD FIRED THE SHOTS THAT WOULD DRAW THE GUARDS to the eastern shore of the island before he launched the invisible boat and sent it on its way. The plan had been to launch the boat first, but he had made a judgement call and decided to fire the gun first because of the storm.

The forecast had been for fog in the area with a thunderstorm staying far from the coast. That storm had shifted and was moving inland with great speed.

The thunder it produced was loud. Henry feared if he had sent the fake boat out to sea too early that the thunder might drown out the sounds it was making.

He felt exposed with the loss of the fog but was still dressed in the garb worn by the guards. If spotted from a distance, he would be mistaken for one of them.

After sending the fake boat on its way, he took off toward the spot where they had left their boat anchored. As he drew closer, he saw that one of the guards had found the craft. If the man reported it, Donahue and the others might split up and he and Tanner would become involved in a firefight before they could make their escape.

Henry couldn't risk shooting the man from where he was. If he missed, the man would fire back at him, and the sound of his weapon could also bring men on the run.

Henry decided to bluff. He was dressed like the guards in a green jumpsuit. His appearance shouldn't place the man on alert until he got a good look at him. It was night and rain was falling. By the time the man saw him up close, it would be too late.

Henry raised up a hand and called out while running towards the guard. "Whose boat is that?"

The guard looked at him while squinting against the rain. "It looks like one of ours, but it shouldn't be here."

Henry had kept running, had sped up, and was charging at the guard before the man could realize something was wrong. Henry tackled him and they wound up in the surf together with the guard on his back. Henry recognized the guard from his previous visit to the island. He had nothing personal against the man and hoped to make his death a swift one. He smashed the guard repeatedly on the side of the head with an elbow to stun him into unconsciousness, then he freed his knife. The six-inch blade cut through the man's jumpsuit and sank into the soft flesh below the hem of the bulletproof vest he was wearing.

As Henry stabbed him, the guard's lips parted, and a sigh escaped, but his eyes remained closed. Henry removed the man's weapon and saw that it was a Glock with a custom grip made of ivory. It was a distinctive weapon, so he placed it in the boat as a spoil of war. It was then that he noticed how turbulent the sea had become. They were in for a rough trip back to the mainland.

The dying guard's body was tossed onto the shore by a huge wave. The man would soon be dead from massive internal bleeding.

Henry tumbled into the bobbing boat and had to struggle

to keep his feet beneath him. Lightning flashed overhead and the sound of the thunder was raucous. Henry kept his head on a swivel as he fought to see through what had become a driving rain. If Tanner was being pursued when he showed up, Henry would provide backup. The green jumpsuit was heavy with the water it absorbed, so Henry shed it to reveal the wet suit he wore beneath it. Because the wet suit was black and covered most of his body, he was difficult to see in the gloom and with the heavy rain.

That effect was lessened when he slid into an auto-inflatable life vest, which was blue. Henry deemed it necessary given the rough sea, and he readied one to hand off to Tanner. If the boat capsized or took on too much water, wearing the vests would lessen their chances of drowning.

When Henry realized that trying to hit a target from the rocking boat would be a waste of time, he clambered out of it and back onto the beach. He thought of the simple fluke anchor holding the boat in place and wondered how much longer it would last, as the height of the waves increased.

Henry wiped water from his eyes as he whispered, "C'mon Tanner," and awaited the arrival of his mentor.

DONAHUE HAD REACHED THE EASTERN SHORE ON A DEAD RUN and saw three of the guards pointing out at the water. He'd been about to ask them what they were doing when he heard a boat. It was difficult to tell where the sound was coming from with the thunder increasing in volume. It was obvious that the boat was near, but Donahue was damned if he could see it.

Another man called from nearby. He had discovered the bodies of the two dead guards who had been out on patrol. He called to Donahue.

"The bastards killed Simmons and Lowry."

"Why do you think it was more than one man?" Donahue asked.

The guard pointed down at the sand and shined the beam of a flashlight on it. "I see two sets of footprints. It looks like they're wearing boots."

Donahue jumped to the conclusion Tanner had been hoping for. He assumed that unknown attackers had come onto the island intent to kill Bergman, only to meet resistance and have to engage in a gun battle. Knowing others would respond, they had decided to give up and flee.

Donahue raised a hand and pointed toward the direction of the dock. "All of you follow me. We're getting in the boats and going after them."

THE ADDITIONAL GUARDS DONAHUE HAD ORDERED BE SENT TO the house walked off the nearby path only moments after Tanner had killed Alex Bergman. They had their rifles up and ready having heard the muffled sound of the suppressed shots that ended Bergman's life.

Seeing their employer lying dead in the rain seized their attention for an instant, it was an instant Tanner used to get off the first shot. His round struck one of the men in the leg. It had been a hurried shot that was fired as Tanner dove to the ground.

He was behind Bergman's corpse and using it as a platform to prop his arms on as he continued to fire at the men. Bergman's body absorbed several bullets before one of the guard's rounds struck Tanner. The bullet carved a groove across the outside of his left boot. He felt his foot go numb. As that was happening, thunder boomed overhead, and night was turned into day by a huge flash of lightning.

One guard was down while the other was wounded but still in the fight. That ended when a round struck him in the forehead.

Tanner stood; the initial numbness in his foot had been replaced by a searing pain. He tried to ignore it as he changed magazines while closing in on the guard with the leg wound. The wound was a mortal one, as the guard's femoral artery had been severed. His blood mixed with the rain and left him lying in a puddle of red.

The guard was alive but fading fast. He stared up at Tanner, laughed once, then his eyes rolled back into his head. Laughing was an odd reaction for a dying man to have, unless that man knew his murderer was about to join him in death.

Tanner dived to the left while turning over and landed on his back on the wet grass. The move saved his life. There was another guard. The man had fired at the spot where Tanner had been and was moving his rifle downward to release more rounds. He never got the chance, as Tanner hammered him with five rounds. Two of those bullets hit flesh. One in the throat and the other destroyed a collarbone.

The sound of the shots had been drowned out by a clap of thunder that was loud enough to rattle the windows in the house.

Tanner made it to his feet again and was unable to ignore the pain in his foot. When he looked down at his boot, he saw blood leaking out where the bullet had ripped it open. As uncomfortable as the minor wound was, he found that he could walk without limping, although the pain was distracting. He took the time to remove his boot to evaluate the wound. It wasn't bad, but it bled a lot. He applied a combat bandage to stop the flow of blood.

With that done, he took off toward the shore to meet Henry at the boat.

~

DONAHUE WAS FILLED WITH FRUSTRATION AS HE HUNG ON tight to a strap in a rocking boat with one hand while trying to use his satellite phone with the other.

The new guards weren't answering their phones and the men who should have been patrolling were nowhere in sight. What he was also failing to see was the boat they were chasing, although they could hear its outboard motors.

Donahue was beginning to wonder if they were in pursuit of some type of submersible like a Seabob. It didn't seem possible as the engine sound was too loud. Whatever it was, they were closing in on it; the boat they were in had more power than what they were chasing.

A minute later, and one of the two men in the boat with him pointed to the starboard side. "I see something!"

The man was shouting, but Donahue couldn't make out his words over the sound of the engines, a noisy bilge pump, and the loud thunder. He looked in the direction the man was pointing and saw a strange sight. It was a machine of some type; the sounds they had heard were coming out of it. Donahue lit it up with a strong beam of light as they came up alongside it. When they struck the crest of a wave, Donahue lost his grip on the searchlight and nearly fell overboard.

In anger, he brought around his rifle, which was hanging on a sling, and fired at the object in the water. Its motor died along with the speakers that had been making the sounds of a fleeing boat. As they began circling it, the device took on water and sank from view. It had all been a diversion to send them off in the wrong direction, or worse, to keep them occupied while an attempt was made on Bergman's life.

Donahue pointed toward Driftwood Island while shouting to the man at the helm. "Get us back to the island!"

The man nodded his understanding and turned the boat

around. When Donahue called Bergman and his friend failed to answer, he got a hollow feeling in the pit of his stomach.

TANNER ARRIVED AT THE BOAT WITHOUT MEETING ANY MORE resistance and smiled when he saw Henry. After catching sight of the dead guard lying on shore, he knew his apprentice had dealt with his own unexpected trouble.

A glance back over his shoulder assured him that no one was on his trail. Henry greeted him with a grin and a question.

"Bergman?"

"He's dead."

"Awesome. Let's get the hell out of here before this storm gets any worse."

Henry climbed into the boat while Tanner slipped out of his jumpsuit. He was at the side of the boat and holding his rifle up with both hands to pass to Henry when a bolt of lightning struck.

Tanner saw a brilliant flash and agony rippled throughout his body. He collapsed into the water as he lost consciousness.

In the boat, Henry had registered seeing the lightning hit the rifle Tanner was handing off to him before he too was felled by a surge of pain. He hadn't been touching the rifle as Tanner had, but his hands had been reaching for it. He tumbled backwards into the boat while losing the struggle to stay conscious, as the storm increased, and thunder continued to reverberate across the horizon.

22

DAZED AND CONFUSED

DONAHUE AND THE MEN WITH HIM MADE IT BACK TO THE DOCK on Driftwood Island, but it had been a struggle to get there. The storm was directly over the area and the sea was turbulent. One of the men on the other boat had fallen overboard. He was rescued when a guard extended a boat hook and snagged the collar of his jumpsuit.

When they did reach the dock, Donahue leapt off the boat and dashed toward the house with five of the men following behind, while the other men were left to secure the boats.

Donahue's heart sank when he saw the front door sitting open, then he took in the sight of the bodies scattered about. All but one of them was dressed in a green jumpsuit. That one was his friend, Alex Bergman.

Donahue rushed over with the hope that Bergman might somehow still be alive. That hope died when he saw the brains leaking out the rear of Bergman's skull.

Tanner came to and rolled onto his side to cough up the seawater he'd taken in while senseless. The pain he was feeling had brought him back to consciousness. The storm was still raging and had increased in its ferocity.

When he was done hacking up water, he fell onto his back again. A moan escaped his lips as he opened his eyes, then he turned over to keep the rain from pelting his face. He had collapsed in the water when the lightning had hit him, but the waves had washed him onto shore. He wound up eight feet to the right of the body of the dead guard Henry had killed.

As his awareness expanded, he sat up and looked at his hands. They were reddened and covered in blisters. The rest of his body ached as well; he felt like he had been sunburned all over. When he tried to curl his fingers, nothing happened, although the thumb on his right hand did twitch.

The wet suit he wore was tattered. During the instant the lightning struck, it had heated the moisture between the suit and Tanner's skin, turning his perspiration into steam and swelling the wet suit's material until areas of it popped like overinflated balloons.

He sat there in the sand looking around in confusion. For the life of him he couldn't remember how he had gotten where he was, nor did he recall being struck by lightning. Looking out at the water he saw only a turbulent sea and crashing waves. The boat he had been about to climb into was gone, but he could not recall it, and so he didn't miss it.

As he watched the high waves pound the sand and flow toward him, he realized he couldn't hear the sound they made. He went to snap his fingers and couldn't because of his injured hands. He then spoke out loud and was unable to hear the words. He was deaf. The realization staggered him, and he again wondered what had happened.

Instinct and a desire to be out of the rain guided him to

get to his feet to head beneath the cover of the trees. When he stood, he felt the ache in his left foot. The bandage was still there, while his other foot wore his one remaining sock, but his boots were missing. The pain in his left foot, and the soreness of his skin was nothing compared to the agony his hands were emitting.

When he spotted the dead man lying in the sand a few feet away a name came to mind.

Henry.

Was that the dead man's name? And if so, why did he know it?

He shook his head and walked toward the trees where there was a degree of shelter from the hard rain. After he settled his back against the trunk of a pine tree, he tried to recall what had happened, but he was too disoriented to concentrate and the agony pulsating from his hands wasn't helping.

When the alarm back at the compound cut off, he wasn't aware of it because of his hearing loss. He also couldn't recall that there were men nearby who would love to kill him.

DONAHUE HAD ORDERED THE ALARM TO BE SHUT OFF. HE WAS still staring down at the body of his friend and employer, Alex Bergman. If not for the rain, his tears would have been obvious to those around him.

I failed you. Donahue thought. Bergman had been relying on him to keep him safe and now he was dead.

One of the remaining guards returned from checking out the house. When he reported that there was no damage done to the steel door or the locks on Bergman's bedroom, Donahue wore a puzzled expression.

Why did you leave your room, Alex? Had you stayed there you might still be alive.

The man who'd been assigned to guard the bedroom door was dead, as were five other guards. That caused Donahue to wonder if they were dealing with more than two people.

He wondered if Echo and her unknown accomplice had returned with help to take another shot at killing Bergman. It didn't seem likely. If they'd had something gimmicky like that fake boat, they would have used it during their first attempt to kill Bergman.

No. Someone else killed Bergman. Someone who'd outsmarted him.

Donahue made a sound born of rage as his hands balled into fists. He turned to speak to the remaining guards.

"Move the bodies into the storage shed for now. When you're done, come into the house for the night. We'll wait out this storm and search the island in the morning."

The guards went to work carrying out their orders and Donahue trudged inside the house to pour a stiff drink.

"BERGMAN... THE CONTRACT—HENRY!" TANNER SAID ALOUD. The confusion caused by the lightning strike was lifting and his mind was growing clear. He had been struck by lightning as he was about to climb into the boat to leave the island for good. The bad luck that had plagued the contract was continuing even after the target was dead. He patted at an ear with the back of a hand and heard nothing. He had read of cases of people going deaf after being struck by lightning; some recovered their hearing; some had been rendered permanently deaf.

He left the cover of the trees and headed to the beach to search for the boat Henry had been in. He saw nothing, as before, then began walking along the shoreline while keeping near the trees in hope of locating it.

It was rough going. His body ached and felt stiff. He was weakened so much by his ordeal that the gusts of wind threatened to knock him over more than once.

He came across the bodies of the men he and Henry had killed earlier, then saw headlights off in the distance as a vehicle approached. Hope flared within him as he thought it might be Henry out looking for him, although, that didn't seem likely.

When he reached for the gun that was strapped to his hip, he found he couldn't bend his fingers enough to grip it. And when he touched the gun the pain in his hand spiked to a new level. He might as well have been unarmed for all the good the gun would do him, or nearly any other weapon for that matter.

He moved behind a tree and laid on the ground in time to avoid being seen as a pickup truck came along the sand. There were two of the guards inside. They parked the truck and got out of it.

Tanner watched as they loaded the corpses of their comrades into the bed of the pickup. They worked silently with shoulders hunched against the driving rain. When they rode off the way they had come, Tanner continued his exploration until he had circled the island and found no trace of Henry or the boat.

Henry wouldn't have left him unless he had no choice. Tanner's only memory of the lightning was its brilliant flash and the agony it spawned. He did recall that Henry was close by. It was possible the lightning had injured him as well.

If so, he might have been knocked unconscious, or worse, and the storm had loosened the grip their anchor had, causing the boat to drift out to sea.

Tanner wore a grim expression as he wondered what fate

had befallen his protégé. He could do nothing to help him in his current condition. And even if he could search for him on the sea it was doubtful he would find him.

Fate had dealt them both a cruel hand. He could only hope Henry somehow survived.

Exhausted, in pain, and with a heavy heart, Tanner trudged to the area where driftwood and other debris washed ashore on the island. The precautions he had taken earlier were proving to be necessary as he squirmed beneath a large, overturned skiff that offered shelter from the rain.

The food and water he had left there earlier were a blessing, as the lightning strike had him feeling dehydrated. It hurt like hell to hold the water bottle between the burnt palms of his hands, and he had to use his teeth to remove the cap, but the water quenched his thirst and made him feel better.

Despite his exhausted state, sleep didn't come quickly. Eventually, exhaustion won out and Tanner slept.

The contract was fulfilled, but he was injured, deafened, and trapped on an island with men who would love to see him dead. And as for Henry, his fate was still unknown.

23
DISASTROUS

DONAHUE WAS IN THE LIVING ROOM AND LOOKING AT VIDEO that had been recorded by the security cameras inside the house. The video displayed the scene outside Bergman's bedroom but had no sound. The guard on duty appeared calm and Donahue saw no sign that an intruder was nearby.

He was astonished to see Bergman rush from his room with a panicked look on his face. He was further shocked by the guard's reaction. Donahue had thought Bergman fled the room because someone had gained entry through the patio doors. But if that had happened, the guard would have raised his rifle and entered the bedroom to deal with the threat. Instead of doing that, the guard followed Bergman over to the stairs. Neither man glanced behind them but only kept running.

A second video gave a view of the home's foyer. Someone must have fired a gun from out of view because the guard was struck and killed by two rounds.

As for Bergman, he had continued his mad rush to flee the house. Donahue paused the video at a point where

Bergman was last visible. The panic displayed on his friend's face was palpable.

Why the hell did you leave the safety of your room, Alex?

Other video showed a figure dressed like one of the guards killing the two men on the porch. Their bodies were found along with three other guards, and Bergman. One of those guards had been the man who'd been watching the video monitors. He must have gone to the house after viewing Bergman's mad dash.

Donahue watched it all again, and again had the same question. *What made you leave your room, Alex? What?*

He could think of no answer that made sense. But he vowed to himself that he would find his friend's killers and make them suffer before they died.

HENRY HAD REGAINED CONSCIOUSNESS TO DISCOVER THAT THE boat was no longer anchored and had drifted away from the island. The small craft was being tossed about in the tempestuous sea as if it were a cork.

Unlike Tanner, his only injury had been the shock he'd received from being so close to the lightning strike. That jolt of electricity had scrambled his nervous system and rendered him unconscious. Had he been touching the rifle as Tanner had been, he might have suffered the same damage to his hands and hearing.

Henry was lying in three inches of water. The boat's bilge pump was inadequate to keep up with the torrent pouring from the sky and water spilling into the boat from the high waves. When he sat up he received a surprise as he saw that the boat was headed toward land. It was one of the many small islands that had no name and was no larger than a football field. Henry sprang to his feet to take the helm only to be thrown backwards and end up in the water.

He spat out seawater as the life vest he wore inflated automatically. Unable to prevent it from happening, all Henry could do was watch as the boat ran aground. The small island had a rocky shore that did the boat's hull no favors and the craft's motors were ripped away from the stern. The boat had made its last sea voyage.

Henry was carried to the same spot by the waves and had his vest punctured by a sharp rock, while another one ripped open his wet suit at the side of his right calf.

He crawled onto shore and beyond the reach of the waves to collapse onto his back. When a bolt of lightning lit up the sky above him, he scrambled to his feet and looked around for shelter. There was none; however, there was a section of rock that jutted out several feet giving the cavity of space beneath it the appearance of a shallow cave. Henry settled there and found that it kept most of the rain off him.

He was only inside the space for a minute when he remembered he had a satellite phone. The thing was dead, having been killed from being exposed to water. Henry left his shelter to climb into the shipwrecked boat and retrieve supplies. There was a bag that contained water, food, and ammunition. It was all dry because the bag was watertight. Henry took it back to his small cave along with a case that held a disassembled sniper rifle.

He shivered as he sat with his back against a stone wall and thought about Tanner. His mentor had taken the brunt of the lightning strike because he'd been holding on to a metal rifle. As tough as Tanner was, the lightning had to have done some damage. And on top of that, the man had been standing in water that was past his waist. If he'd been rendered unconscious, he might have drowned.

Henry braved the elements once more to attempt to get

his bearings. He climbed up a hill and looked around. He saw little until a flash of lightning illuminated the sky. As that was happening, Henry spotted the silhouette of a tower off in the distance to his left. He was confused until he realized what it was he had seen. It wasn't a tower; it was the ancient lighthouse on Driftwood Island. Henry had gotten a close-up look at it when he'd been on the island as a guard.

A rough estimate placed him five miles away from Driftwood. In normal weather he could swim there. Given how many small islands were in the area, he wouldn't have to make the trip nonstop, but could rest along the way.

But not in the present conditions. If he attempted to swim during the storm he would likely drown, lose his way, or be taken out by an undercurrent that might sweep him far out to sea.

Henry saw no option other than to return to the shelter of the cave and wait out the storm. He could begin a search for Tanner when the sea was calmer and there was daylight.

Henry was worried about Tanner. He also knew that if anyone could survive what had happened it would be his exceptional mentor. Then again, surviving the lightning strike and the storm weren't Tanner's only problems. Donahue and his remaining guards were another concern. If they found Tanner before he did, and in a weakened state, it could be disastrous.

24
HIDE AND SURVIVE

DONAHUE GREETED THE SIGHT OF THE SUNRISE WITH A SIGH. He was standing in the home's living room and looking out a bay window. He'd been up all night drinking coffee laced with whiskey, but hadn't imbibed enough liquor to get drunk, only enough to dull the pain of his loss.

Alex Bergman was dead. His only friend was dead, and he had failed him.

Donahue heard a noise behind him; he turned to see two of the surviving guards. They had taken off the green jumpsuits and had on tactical vests. Each man held a rifle and there were weapons strapped to their hips.

The taller of the men gestured to his friend. "Gary and I got to talking; we think there's a chance the men who killed our friends and Mr. Bergman might still be nearby."

Donahue wrinkled his brow in confusion. "Why would they be?"

"You were out in that storm last night. We barely made it back here without capsizing. We think the killers might have had trouble and waited the storm out on one of the smaller islands."

Donahue considered that idea and liked it. If true, it meant he might be able to get revenge. And yeah, it made sense. The storm had been a beast and had moved into the area with unexpected speed. He also wanted to know what had happened to the new guards on the nearby island. They still weren't answering their phones.

"I'll come search with you, but first I'll tell the other men to begin a search here. If Alex's killer didn't make it off the island, that would mean he's in hiding somewhere."

~

TANNER WAS IN HIDING. HE WAS ALSO FEELING BETTER. HIS hearing wasn't normal, but it was returning, as had his strength. When he had awakened, he had heard the sharp cries made by the gulls that were nearby. The sound was fainter than it should be, but nonetheless, he had heard them. That meant his hearing loss wasn't permanent, although his hands still ached, and he was unable to bend his fingers enough to grip his weapon.

There was one weapon he could use if it became necessary; it was an explosive device he had brought along as part of his due diligence. The gadget could be armed by entering a four-digit combination of numbers that would cause it to explode seconds later. If he were forced to use it, conditions would be dire. He could activate it, but he wouldn't be able to toss it far, since he couldn't grip it. That would mean he might still be inside the explosive's blast radius when the device went off. Not an ideal situation.

Tanner slid out from beneath the overturned skiff and looked about at the beginning of what would be a beautiful day. With the passage of the storm, the sky was blue, and clouds were absent. The wind remained; it made the trees sway.

After urinating, Tanner moved into the waves and let them wash the sand from his back and his hair. He had to be on the move despite the risk it posed if he were spotted.

Henry was missing. Tanner intended to steal one of the boats and go looking for him. He had to know what had happened to his friend.

Not wanting to leave fresh footprints behind in the sand, Tanner walked along the shore where the waves would wipe away the evidence of his passing. He was forced to move slowly because of the wet sand sucking at his bare feet and the need to continually pause and look around. Even if his hearing had been perfect, he would have been at a disadvantage because of the sound made by the crashing waves.

As he neared the dock, he saw that two of the boats were already out on the water. He hoped that was Donahue and the remaining guards leaving the island for good, but that was not how his luck had been going, not during this contract. It was more likely that the men were out searching for him and Henry.

Tanner increased his pace toward the boats that remained. He had to find Henry before anyone else did.

He turned his head to look behind him and saw movement. Two men were coming out of the trees a hundred yards behind him. Tanner gave the boats a mournful look. He had no chance to get one underway before the men would reach him.

One of the men raised an arm to point at him as the other took a knee and brought a rifle up to his shoulder. Tanner dropped into the surf as the gun was fired. The sound was barely discernible to his damaged ears.

Knowing he couldn't stay out in the open and that the shot would alert anyone else nearby that there was trouble, Tanner jetted toward the cover of the trees. A sapling in front of him splintered from the impact of a bullet and he kept running.

He had to get out of sight and wait for another opportunity to steal a boat. He wouldn't do Henry any good if he were captured. If he could make it back to the debris field where the overturned skiff was, he could use it as a shelter again. The problem with that was that he would leave footprints in the sand to reach it, unless he approached it from the side that was near the water. To do that, he'd have to cross an open area of beach, and that would also leave footprints behind.

He had readied a second place to take shelter in on the previous day when he'd been doing his due diligence. If he could reach that spot without being seen, there was a chance he could stay hidden for hours. His new hiding place would be inside one of the pits Donahue had ordered the men to dig along the trails as a trap. Tanner had investigated one the day before and saw that there was room to sit next to the concealed wooden spikes. He had deposited additional food and bottles of water there as well.

However, getting into the space was easier than getting out, because he couldn't curl his damaged fingers to use for climbing. Tanner had to risk it. He would think of a way to extricate himself from the pit when the time came.

Tanner reached his new hiding spot, slid aside the thin, sand-covered sheet of wood covering the pit, and lowered himself into it. Unable to dig his fingers into the dirt wall to get a grip, he stretched out his legs and pressed his feet against the side of the walls, then used his blistered palms to balance himself against the wall he was facing. The pain was agony, and so he switched to using his forearms instead.

He needed to slide the wood back in place to make the trap appear undisturbed. His head accomplish that. By moving the board along with the crown of his head, he was able to push it back into position. When it was done, he had to let himself drop into the dark space while being careful to slide along the wall and avoid the spikes. The effort had made his hands ache with renewed vigor and caused him to break out in a sweat.

Once again, he was safe and hidden from sight, as he sat inside the dark space. But what about Henry? Was he injured somewhere, or had he drowned the night before?

Tanner shook his head, dismissing the idea. Henry wasn't a Tanner yet, but the boy had what it took to be one and he had already been trained to a high degree. If the lightning strike hadn't killed him, he would continue to survive, and Donahue and his men wouldn't stand a chance against him.

25

BLACK AS THE PIT FROM POLE TO POLE

DONAHUE HAD SENT TWO MEN OFF IN ONE BOAT TO SEARCH for their attackers while he and another man traveled to the island where the new guards were based.

Henry had left the small cave where he'd spent the night and had swum to the next nearest isle. As he rested there before resuming his journey to Driftwood Island, he had heard the approach of the boat with the two guards in it. He stayed hidden as the boat went past him. From where they were on the water, Henry knew they would soon spot his damaged runabout.

He had slipped back into the water and swam the way he had traveled. After spotting his boat, the two men would likely drop anchor and at least one of them would go ashore to investigate. If they did that, Henry would have a chance to take their boat.

∾

DONAHUE DISCOVERED THE BODIES OF THE NEW GUARDS. SOME of the men were missing, as the storm had swept their corpses out to sea.

As he was taking in the carnage, he received two calls. The guards remaining on the island had spotted one of Bergman's assassins and were hunting him down. The second call came from the men who were out searching the area. They had found a damaged boat that had run ashore one of the tiny islands. There was proof that the boat had been at Driftwood Island because a gun had been found on it that had belonged to a slain guard; it was a Glock with an ivory grip.

The news cheered Donahue some. Alex Bergman was dead, but there remained the chance that his death would be avenged. He spoke into his satellite phone.

"Tell the men there's a ten-thousand-dollar reward to whoever captures Mr. Bergman's killers. That's ten thousand for each of the killers you capture alive. Five thousand if they're dead."

The man said he would spread the word and Donahue headed back to Driftwood Island. Once he had his hands on the bastard who had killed his friend, he would take great pleasure in torturing that man for hours.

ONE OF THE MEN WORKING FOR DONAHUE WAS AN Englishman named Andrew who was an avid hunter and tracker. He had picked up Tanner's trail and it led him to the boobytrapped walkway.

Andrew smiled. *You're a clever bastard. I never would have thought of looking down in that hole if I hadn't tracked you here.*

He moved some distance away so he could call for backup without being overheard by the man hiding in the pit.

Andrew had been about to use his radio when a voice came in over it informing everyone about the reward being offered.

That made Andrew change his mind about asking for help. If someone helped him, he would have to share the reward money with them. He went back to the pit that had been dug along the trail and used the tip of his rifle barrel to slide aside one of the boards that covered it. When he saw Tanner gazing up at him and blinking against the sudden light in his eyes, he ordered him to show his hands. Instead of shouting, Andrew spoke softly, so that none of the other guards who might be nearby could hear him. If they came over now, they might later claim they were part of the capture. Andrew didn't want to alert anyone until he had Tanner out of the pit and with his wrists bound behind his back.

Because of his compromised hearing, Tanner hadn't been aware of Andrew's presence until the board above his head moved and light began filling the pit. He had a loaded gun but couldn't use it against Andrew due to his damaged hands. If the man was out to kill him, there would be nothing he could do if he started shooting that rifle off.

Climbing into the pit to hide had been a risk, but he would have been at greater peril had he stayed out in the open where men had been shooting at him.

Tanner saw Andrew's lips move and heard his words, but they were at too low a volume for him to make out. Still, he had read his lips and understood what he wanted. He raised his hands in surrender as a bid to buy time. Andrew's expression changed as he took in the sight of his burnt palms and tattered wet suit.

"What happened to you?"

"I was struck by lightning."

"Good for you, you bastard. You deserve all the pain you can get for killing my mates and Mr. Bergman. Now, climb on out of there."

"I can't climb; my fingers won't bend more than a little, but I can use my legs to get out."

"Your legs? What do you mean?"

"I'll show you."

Tanner bent down as far as he could and felt the nearest spike press against his back. He shot his feet out as he sprang upward and wound up doing a full split with his feet pressed against the side walls of the pit. He was leaning forward with his elbows against the wall in front of him. If he fell backwards, he would be impaled by several spikes.

Tanner began inching one foot up a wall and then the other as he headed toward the top.

Despite the animosity Andrew felt toward Tanner, he was impressed by his display of athleticism and balance, and it showed in his expression and words.

"You're one fit bastard, aren't you?"

Tanner continued his ascent until he was at the top and able to rest his upper body on the lip of the pit. When his feet had also reached the top edges of the walls they had climbed, he was no longer in danger of falling backwards. He bent his knees while using his forearms to flip himself over onto his back.

Andrew had been holding his rifle pointed at the ground, he aimed at Tanner when he spotted the gun holstered on his hip.

"Take that gun out slowly and toss it away."

Tanner held up his hands again as he made it to his feet. "If I could grip the weapon, I would have threatened you with it already."

"Oh, yeah, I guess. But I still don't like you having a weapon. Turn around and I'll take it from you."

Tanner turned his back on Andrew and looked down. He couldn't hear the man's movements, but he could tell where he was and the position of the rifle by the shadows they cast. When Andrew switched the rifle to his left hand and reached out with his right to grab Tanner's gun, the hit man made his move.

Tanner dropped onto his forearms while kicking his feet out behind him. One foot struck Andrew in a knee while the other found his groin. Andrew fell sideways and landed on top of Tanner. Tanner sent an elbow into his face and connected with an eye, causing Andrew to release a shout of pain. While supporting himself with his forearms, Tanner straightened his legs to raise his lower back. Andrew, still lying across him, began to roll toward the edge of the pit.

"No! No!" Andrew cried as he realized what was happening. He released the rifle and tried to grab onto Tanner. There was little to grab hold of since the wet suit Tanner wore was skintight. Andrew tumbled into the pit while screaming but the sound ended abruptly. A spike had entered his left ear and came out the other side of his head.

Other shouts could be heard as the rest of the guards called to each other. Tanner's recovering ears could detect the sounds, but he was having trouble determining what direction they were coming from.

He was back in the trees and headed away from the pit. Once again on the run and looking for a new place to hide.

2 6
IN THE NICK OF TIME

HENRY HAD SNUCK UP ON THE MEN FROM THE SEARCH BOAT and used his silenced gun to silence them forever. One of the men was still holding a satellite phone in his dead hand. He had just reported in and told Donahue that he and his companion would continue to search.

Along with that communication had come the news that Tanner was still alive and being hunted down on Driftwood Island. Henry was worried for his mentor's safety but was overjoyed to know that Tanner still lived.

He found the keys to the boat on a chain that was hanging around one of the dead men's necks. Along with that he took the man's satellite phone and the waterproof case that had been used during the swim from the boat. The case had a strap and could be worn around the neck.

Henry swam out to the boat as fast as he could, eager to get underway and aid Tanner. He did have to make one stop to the other island where he had left the case containing the sniper rifle. He had a feeling he was going to need it.

Donahue was back on Driftwood Island and leading the search for Tanner. He had three teams consisting of two men each working a grid pattern to find Tanner. He was working along with them with two more of the guards at his side.

Andrew's body had been discovered in the pit and had enraged the guards, as the Englishman had been well-liked. It puzzled Donahue as to why Tanner hadn't claimed Andrew's rifle. Tanner undoubtably had a gun of his own, but the rifle was a formidable weapon to have. If nothing else, it would have given him more firepower. Being outnumbered, Tanner couldn't have too much ammunition.

The men he'd sent out to search the small islands had found a damaged boat along with signs that someone had survived the wreck. That meant that at least two men had been responsible for killing Bergman.

Donahue ached to get his hands on both men. He quivered with anticipation whenever he thought about what he would do to them once he had the assassins at his mercy. There would be no mercy, no compassion, only a long, slow, excruciating death.

A shout came over the two-way radio. It was from one of the guards searching the shoreline for footprints.

"This is Murphy. Joe Kelly is dead! He went to take a leak in the trees and when he didn't come right back, I went looking for him. It looks like someone broke his neck."

Donahue keyed his radio. "Tell us where you are, Murphy, and we'll all converge on that area. It's time to hunt this bastard down."

Tanner had come up behind the guard named Joe Kelly as the man had been urinating. He couldn't use his hands well, but there was nothing wrong with his arms. He had wrapped his left arm across Kelly's face and locked his wrist behind Kelly's neck. At the same time, he shoved his right arm down the front of the man's green jumpsuit. As his right arm used the jumpsuit to wrench the man's torso one way, his left arm jerked Kelly's head in the other direction. He was rewarded by a popping sound as Kelly's neck broke. That sound signified both the man's impending death and the fact that his hearing had improved further.

The dying man represented one less threat and one less chance to die.

Tanner had stepped over Kelly's body while it was still twitching and headed toward the area that had given the island its name. He was hoping to set up a trap that would lure all the remaining men to him so he could use the explosive device he had. If it worked, they would all be wounded or dead. To do so, he would have to risk his own life, as he could only toss the disk so far using an open palm. He would have to hope that the debris he would take cover behind would be enough to shield him from the blast.

It wasn't a great plan, but he knew he could only avoid a bullet for so long as outnumbered as he was. Tanner left the trees and sprinted across the sand to leave a trail for his pursuers. He was the prey, but he hoped to turn the tables and become a predator.

ONE OF THE GUARDS SPOTTED TANNER'S FOOTPRINTS IN THE sand and alerted his partner. When they followed the tracks to the debris field and saw no fresh footprints leading away, they were confident they had their man trapped.

A guard radioed Donahue as the other kept watch. Donahue and the remaining guards came running to the scene with their rifles in their hands.

A mustached guard named Hobbs pointed toward the mound of driftwood that was mixed in with damaged boats and other debris.

"We need to be careful how we go about this. The man has a gun, and he could try sniping at us from within that stack of junk."

"There are eight of us," Donahue said. "We can flush him out by firing into the pile."

"Didn't you say you wanted this guy alive?"

"I'd prefer it, yeah, so I can torture the bastard."

Hobbs smiled. "I know a way we can force him out into the open."

TANNER WAS ON THE OTHER SIDE OF THE PILE AND HIDDEN beneath the skiff he'd slept under the night before. He had one side of the boat propped up with a three-inch chunk of wood that allowed him to peer out. When Donahue and the others came near. he would see their feet. When they were close enough, he would activate the explosive device he had, toss it out at the men, then push aside the chunk of wood and let the skiff fall over him.

The weather worn wood of the old skiff would be all that stood between him and the projectiles that would head his way, along with the force generated by the blast. It was a weak shield, and one that would leave him vulnerable, but it might be enough to prevent him from suffering a mortal injury. Maybe.

Tanner had heard the murmur of voices and knew that the men were nearby, but they had yet to come into view. He realized why that was when he caught the scent of burning wood. He eased out from beneath the skiff and a hot ember singed the back of his neck.

Donahue wasn't walking into his trap; he had decided to set fire to the debris field and force Tanner out into the open. It was a good plan. Tanner had a choice of burning to death or revealing himself.

He looked down at the disk in his right hand and knew it was still his only chance. He was about to poke at the buttons that would set it to go off when he heard the first shot. It sounded like a high-powered rifle.

DONAHUE STOOD BACK FROM THE FIRE HE'D SET AND WATCHED the flames consume the detritus washed ashore by the sea. He'd had to use the fluid from a cigarette lighter to start the blaze on a dry section of wood, given how wet the outer layer of the pile was.

His eyes flicked from left to right as he waited for the hit man he hunted to show himself.

The guy couldn't stay hidden among the stacks of debris much longer or he risked burning to death. Hobbs was on his left. Donahue heard him grunt an instant before he registered the sound of the shot that killed the man. Hobbs had been hit between the shoulder blades and had a huge exit wound where his sternum had been.

The other men spun around to return fire at their attacker and saw no one, then another man went down, followed by a third.

The fire was producing a great deal of gray smoke that the wind was blowing toward the trees. Donahue dived, rolled, and found concealment within the smoke.

The shots continued one after the other. Judging by the screams and the grunts of pain, the shooter never missed his mark.

Who the hell is shooting at us?

~

HENRY HAD COME ASHORE IN HIS STOLEN BOAT AND BEGAN HIS search for Tanner. He'd been hidden from view behind a wall when he'd heard two passing guards talking about having someone trapped near the debris field. He followed and saw that Donahue still had seven men left. If he was going to triumph over those odds, he needed an advantage. The sniper rifle gave him that, but he would be standing out in the open and within range of the guards' own rifles were he to engage them. If he moved back out of range of them, he would also be out of the line of sight as the shoreline curved, and unable to make a shot of his own.

When he looked over at the crumbling old lighthouse, he saw the solution. He would have a view of much of the island from the top of the dilapidated structure and be beyond the range of the guard's guns.

With no stairs to climb, Henry scaled the outer wall of the old lighthouse with the sniper rifle strapped to his back. It had been tough going. The weathered stones were wet and moss-covered, and the gusting wind was also a factor. Henry was willing to risk taking a fall if it meant helping Tanner. The man had saved his life more than once and meant more to him than anyone else, apart from his grandmother, Laura.

Henry made it up to the empty chamber where the beacon once shone. The glass was gone along with the reflectors and the lenses that had been used to magnify the light and send it out across the water.

He was shocked to see the fire when he looked out and understood that Donahue was trying to force Tanner into the open so he could kill him.

Henry had lowered himself to his knees, settled the rifle on the windowsill, and began evening the odds.

Hobbs had been the first to die, and the shooting continued.

TANNER GRINNED WHEN HE REALIZED THAT THE SHOTS weren't coming from any of the guards.

Henry! Thank God. The kid is still alive.

Tanner had no choice but to come out into the open because of the heat and the flames of the fire. He still carried the explosive disk in his hand but had yet to arm it.

A scream came from the other side of the flames as Henry continued his assault. There was a burst of return fire that ended when the sniper rifle boomed again. Tanner's hearing was still off but not his eyesight. He spotted the movement of a rifle barrel up in the lighthouse as Henry repositioned to take a shot at a fleeing guard. The rifle boomed once more, and another scream carried on the air.

Tanner was about to raise a hand to wave to Henry when he saw Donahue. The man was using the smoke to conceal his movements as he headed into the cover of the trees.

Tanner went in pursuit.

HENRY SAW A FIGURE MOVE OUT OF THE SMOKE NEAR THE TREE line. He could see the back of a blond head through the rifle scope and assumed he was looking at Donahue. The man was dressed in chinos and a blue long-sleeved shirt instead of the uniform of the guards.

Henry pumped a fist into the air and cried "Yes!" when a black-clad figure ran after Donahue. It was Tanner. Until that moment, Henry couldn't be certain his mentor was alive.

Now he knew he was not only alive but well enough to chase after Donahue.

Below, near the burning debris field, seven men lay in the sand, either dead or dying. Henry had cut them down one after the other with the sniper rifle and never missed a shot.

He tossed the rifle onto his back again and could feel the heat of the freshly used barrel through the wet suit he wore. Climbing down was as difficult as the trip up; Henry had to force himself to take his time and not make a mistake through impatience. If he rushed and fell, he could wind up hurting himself.

However, he threw caution away when he was ten feet off the ground and decided to leap to the sand below. He landed well but suffered a burn to the back of his right ear from the tip of the rifle barrel.

He ignored the sting of the pain and began running to catch up to Tanner.

DONAHUE WAS COUGHING FROM THE SMOKE HE'D INHALED, but his long legs helped him cover a lot of ground. Still, Tanner was faster and in better shape. He was catching up to the man when Donahue skidded to a stop, turned, and brought up his rifle.

Tanner veered left to dive behind the wide base of a tree whose top part had broken off during the storm. Donahue took cover behind his own tree. When Tanner didn't fire at him, Donahue laughed.

"You're out of ammunition, otherwise you would have shot me in the back as you were chasing me."

Tanner said nothing. He was busy programing the explosive disk to go off in five seconds. Instead of trying to toss it toward Donahue, he waited while holding down the button that paused the countdown.

Donahue called to him. "How did you get Alex to leave the house?"

Tanner's hearing was still recovering, and he hadn't made out every word Donahue had said, but he had discerned enough to know what he was asking.

"I called Bergman while pretending to be you and told him there was a bomb about to go off inside the house."

"You're lying! Alex would have known it wasn't my voice."

Tanner cleared his throat, then spoke in a good imitation of Donahue's voice. "Alex, get out of the house. There's a bomb about to go off. Get out now!" He then spoke in his own voice. "How's it feel knowing your friend died while believing you betrayed him?"

Donahue shouted, "You son of a bitch!" and sent three rounds toward Tanner. Pieces of the tree he hid behind went flying as the bullets hit home.

When Tanner didn't return fire, Donahue stepped out into the open. "Your gun is empty."

Tanner made no reply, but he readied himself to toss the disk once Donahue came a little closer. He tried taunting the man again.

"What are you going to do for money now that Bergman is dead? Are you going to play lackey to another scumbag who traffics in women?"

Donahue gritted his teeth in anger as he crept forward with his rifle ready to fire. Tanner removed his finger from the button and let the countdown commence. When there were three seconds left, he tossed the disk toward Donahue, then laid flat behind the tree stump.

DONAHUE GOT OFF A SHOT THAT PASSED BETWEEN TWO fingers on the hand that tossed the disk. When he looked down to see what Tanner had thrown at him, he gasped in understanding when he saw the red numbers on the disk turn from a two to a one. Donahue was bending his knees to dive for cover when the disk exploded. The force of the detonation sent him eight feet through the air and embedded dozens of small projectiles into his back and the rear of his head.

He groaned once, crawled a foot, then collapsed and died.

TANNER ROSE FROM THE GROUND AND WALKED OVER TO CHECK on Donahue. When he heard Henry calling his name, he turned to look at the place where the sound had come from.

There was no one there, but then he spotted Henry a few yards over from where he had called from.

Smart, Tanner thought. Henry had needed to get his attention, but he also couldn't be sure there was no one around who might mean them harm. After calling out his name, Henry had changed his position, in case someone fired at the spot where he had been.

"I'm over here," Tanner said. "Donahue is dead."

Henry came running over with a grin on his face. "You're okay?"

Tanner showed him the palms of his hands. "That lightning left me a little worse for wear. How are you?"

"I'm good, and I took out the remaining guards. I think everyone is dead."

"You saved my life, Henry. If I'd been forced to use that exploding disk against so many men, I might have injured myself or been killed by a survivor."

"I was happy to help; you've saved my life more than once."

During their walk to the dock, Tanner asked Henry what had happened to him after the lightning struck them, then told Henry how he had woken up half-drowned, disoriented, and deafened.

"But you can hear well now, right?"

"It's improving, and so are my hands," Tanner said, as he tried to curl his fingers. He couldn't make a fist yet, but his fingers had regained some range of movement. The important thing was to get the burns treated before the skin on his palms became infected.

When they were on a boat and headed away from the island, Tanner directed Henry to take them north first before heading toward the mainland. The debris fire was burning well, and the smoke might bring the Coast Guard around to investigate. By heading north and coming ashore in a different area, they had a better chance of not running into the authorities.

"I don't care what direction we travel in," Henry said. "So long as it takes us away from that damn island. This contract sucked ass."

Tanner smiled. He couldn't have said it better.

TANNER RETURNS!

Available for pre-order - TANNER: YEAR SIX - On Sale August 31st.

AFTERWORD

Thank you,

REMINGTON KANE

JOIN MY INNER CIRCLE

You'll receive FREE books, such as,

SLAY BELLS – A TANNER NOVEL – BOOK 0

TAKEN! ALPHABET SERIES – 26 ORIGINAL TAKEN! TALES

BLUE STEELE - KARMA

Also – Exclusive short stories featuring TANNER, along with other books.

TO BECOME AN INNER CIRCLE MEMBER, GO TO:
  http://remingtonkane.com/mailing-list/

ALSO BY REMINGTON KANE

The Young Guns Series in order

YOUNG GUNS

YOUNG GUNS 2 - SMOKE & MIRRORS

YOUNG GUNS 3 - BEYOND LIMITS

YOUNG GUNS 4 - RYKER'S RAIDERS

YOUNG GUNS 5 - ULTIMATE TRAINING

YOUNG GUNS 6 - CONTRACT TO KILL

YOUNG GUNS 7 - FIRST LOVE

YOUNG GUNS 8 - THE END OF THE BEGINNING

A Tanner Series in order

TANNER: YEAR ONE

TANNER: YEAR TWO

TANNER: YEAR THREE

TANNER: YEAR FOUR

TANNER: YEAR FIVE

The TAKEN! Series in order

TAKEN! - LOVE CONQUERS ALL - Book 1

TAKEN! - SECRETS & LIES - Book 2

TAKEN! - STALKER - Book 3

TAKEN! - BREAKOUT! - Book 4

TAKEN! - THE THIRTY-NINE - Book 5

TAKEN! - KIDNAPPING THE DEVIL - Book 6

TAKEN! - HIT SQUAD - Book 7

TAKEN! - MASQUERADE - Book 8

TAKEN! - SERIOUS BUSINESS - Book 9

TAKEN! - THE COUPLE THAT SLAYS TOGETHER - Book 10

TAKEN! - PUT ASUNDER - Book 11

TAKEN! - LIKE BOND, ONLY BETTER - Book 12

TAKEN! - MEDIEVAL - Book 13

TAKEN! - RISEN! - Book 14

TAKEN! - VACATION - Book 15

TAKEN! - MICHAEL - Book 16

TAKEN! - BEDEVILED - Book 17

TAKEN! - INTENTIONAL ACTS OF VIOLENCE - Book 18

TAKEN! - THE KING OF KILLERS – Book 19

TAKEN! - NO MORE MR. NICE GUY - Book 20 & the Series
Finale

The MR. WHITE Series

PAST IMPERFECT - MR. WHITE - Book 1

HUNTED - MR. WHITE - Book 2

The UNLEASH Series

TERROR IN NEW YORK - Book 1

THE EXECUTIONER'S MASK - Book 2

The BLUE STEELE Series in order

BLUE STEELE - BOUNTY HUNTER- Book 1

BLUE STEELE - BROKEN- Book 2

BLUE STEELE - VENGEANCE- Book 3

BLUE STEELE - THAT WHICH DOESN'T KILL ME- Book 4

BLUE STEELE - ON THE HUNT- Book 5

BLUE STEELE - PAST SINS - Book 6

BLUE STEELE - DADDY'S GIRL - Book 7 & the Series Finale

The CALIBER DETECTIVE AGENCY Series in order

CALIBER DETECTIVE AGENCY - GENERATIONS- Book 1

CALIBER DETECTIVE AGENCY - TEMPTATION- Book 2

CALIBER DETECTIVE AGENCY - A RANSOM PAID IN BLOOD- Book 3

CALIBER DETECTIVE AGENCY - MISSING- Book 4

CALIBER DETECTIVE AGENCY - DECEPTION- Book 5

CALIBER DETECTIVE AGENCY - CRUCIBLE- Book 6

CALIBER DETECTIVE AGENCY – LEGENDARY – Book 7

CALIBER DETECTIVE AGENCY – WE ARE GATHERED HERE TODAY - Book 8

CALIBER DETECTIVE AGENCY - MEANS, MOTIVE, and OPPORTUNITY - Book 9 & the Series Finale

THE TAKEN!/TANNER Series in order

THE CONTRACT: KILL JESSICA WHITE - Taken!/Tanner - Book 1

UNFINISHED BUSINESS – Taken!/Tanner – Book 2

THE ABDUCTION OF THOMAS LAWSON - Taken!/Tanner – Book 3

PREDATOR - Taken!/Tanner - Book 4

DETECTIVE PIERCE Series in order

MONSTERS - A Detective Pierce Novel - Book 1

DEMONS - A Detective Pierce Novel - Book 2

ANGELS - A Detective Pierce Novel - Book 3

THE OCEAN BEACH ISLAND Series in order

THE MANY AND THE ONE - Book 1

SINS & SECOND CHANES - Book 2

DRY ADULTERY, WET AMBITION -Book 3

OF TONGUE AND PEN - Book 4

ALL GOOD THINGS... - Book 5

LITTLE WHITE SINS - Book 6

THE LIGHT OF DARKNESS - Book 7

STERN ISLAND - Book 8 & the Series Finale

THE REVENGE Series in order

JOHNNY REVENGE - The Revenge Series - Book 1

THE APPOINTMENT KILLER - The Revenge Series - Book 2

AN I FOR AN I - The Revenge Series - Book 3

ALSO

THE EFFECT: Reality is changing!

THE FIX-IT MAN: A Tale of True Love and Revenge

DOUBLE OR NOTHING

PARKER & KNIGHT

REDEMPTION: Someone's taken her

DESOLATION LAKE

TIME TRAVEL TALES & OTHER SHORT STORIES

Made in United States
Orlando, FL
14 August 2022

21020133R00136